"Ca

This w...

Savanna... ...lot. Why would she get off that easily? "Okay."

"Have we met before?"

"No," she said, and even managed a smile. "I don't see how."

"You're not from around here?"

She shook her head. "Nope."

"It's not a line. You really do look familiar."

She shrugged. "I get that a lot."

Mike frowned. "I can't see why," he said, his gaze roaming over her face, lingering on her mouth. "I'm Mike, by the way."

"Savannah." She used her middle name these days, so that should have thrown him. But now he was studying her even closer. "Well, I'd better get back to the table. I promise not to bulldoze over you again."

"No worries. I'm tough," he said with a dazzling smile. It disappeared in the next instant. "I know where I've seen you—"

Dear Reader,

Mike Burnett, the hero of this book, has been on my mind for a long time. The Made in Montana series began in Blaze, and Mike was first mentioned in *Behind Closed Doors*. He did some carpentry work for the heroine in that story, and that might have been it. But he stuck with me. Honorable, reliable, handsome, he kept popping into my thoughts, but I wasn't finding the perfect heroine for him. Then he showed up in *Come Closer, Cowboy*, and would have asked the heroine out, but she was already taken. Mike not only stayed with me, but I was getting worried. He needed someone really special.

Then came Savannah James, along with a great deal of relief. I could stop worrying. No one could be more perfect for him, just like he was for Savannah. Mike had known her as a shy, quiet girl who'd been dealt a harsh blow. Hadn't seen her in years, but when she showed up in Blackfoot Falls, he recognized her right off, and, oh, boy, she remembered him. I'm so pleased to have finally found the perfect woman that a man like Mike deserves...and Savannah is one lucky lady.

Hope you enjoy their story!

All my best,

Debbi Rawlins

HER COWBOY REUNION

Debbi Rawlins

HARLEQUIN® WESTERN ROMANCE

Recycling programs
for this product may
not exist in your area.

ISBN-13: 978-1-335-69955-8

Her Cowboy Reunion

Copyright © 2018 by Debbi Quattrone

Printed in U.S.A.

Debbi Rawlins grew up on the island of Oahu in Hawaii, but always loved Western movies and books. When she was twelve she spent the summer on the Big Island of Hawaii, and had the dubious honor of being thrown off her first horse. A year later, minutes before a parade started down her street, she managed to find the most skittish horse in the lineup and...you can probably guess the rest.

These days, sixty-five-plus books later, she lives on four acres in gorgeous rural Utah surrounded by dogs, cats, goats, chickens and free-range cattle who just love taking down her fence every couple years.

Visit the Author Profile page
at Harlequin.com for more titles.

Chapter One

Elizabeth Savannah James sat in her rental car outside the motel. Somewhere between Denver and Blackfoot Falls, she'd gotten cold feet. Terrified someone would recognize her. Worried her boss would discover she'd been less than truthful.

Well, too bad.

Now wasn't the time to go into a meltdown, she thought as she drew in the clean mountain air.

The whole idea that she was starting to panic was ridiculous, considering it was her choice to come to this small cow town. In fact, she'd lobbied hard for this assignment. No one would remember her or even give her a second look. She'd left Montana at fourteen, and before that she'd been homeschooled and rarely ventured far from her family's cabin. If not for the explosive chain of events that had led to her and her mom fleeing town, Savannah figured most people would barely have been aware of her existence.

That final week, though...

She shuddered.

The scandal had reached every tiny, dark corner of the community and rocked it to its core. But then, her mom had committed one of the most unforgivable sins known to mankind. Or at least to every woman who lived within a hundred miles of Blackfoot Falls. And she hadn't done it just once.

So, after receiving a notice from the bank, they'd packed as much as they could into her mom's shabby two-door compact and then sneaked off sometime before morning light. The little rattletrap had the loudest muffler. Savannah remembered squeezing her eyes shut and covering her ears with both hands until they'd gotten miles away from Blackfoot Falls and all the evil glares.

To a shy, introverted teenager, it had felt as if all eyes were on her, as if every person in the county despised her, and all she'd wanted to do was run as fast as she could.

That fateful day had occurred quite literally half a lifetime ago. Now, at twenty-eight, she looked completely different. Her mousy brown hair was honey blond now, she'd lost the extra ten pounds of baby fat ages ago and she didn't answer to Elizabeth any longer. But best of all, she was successful and enjoying a career she loved.

Just as long as her boss never found out she'd lied. Not outright, but by omission. Porter Burke International had a sterling reputation. No other company was better at community branding and development. That's why Sadie Thompson, the mayor of Blackfoot Falls, had hired them to find a way to attract more tourists.

But first Savannah and her small team of secret shoppers needed to get a fresh take on the place. Playing tourists, they would check into the motel and inn, eat in the restaurants, drink in the bars, shop in the stores and generally partake of everything the town had to offer. Their undercover operation would last five days, and then they'd give a presentation to go over their assessment and suggestions.

A knock on the car window made her jump.

Dammit.

Ron opened her door. "Is this some kind of joke?"

"What do you mean?"

"Did you just get here? Have you driven down Main Street yet?"

Savannah sighed. "Where's Nina? Didn't you two come together?"

"She's checking in at the Boarding House on the other end of town."

"Wait a minute—"

"Move your head an inch to the left. You can probably see it from here," he said, his sarcasm grating on her nerves. "Talk about a one-horse town…it's maybe seven blocks long. They don't even have a traffic light."

"Why aren't you with her? You should be checking in together." They were supposed to be posing as an engaged couple.

"This is ridiculous. Three of us stuck out here for a week? Hell, we could've wrapped this up in a day."

"If you'd read your prep sheet, you'd know that Hollywood has taken an interest in the area. They've been shooting films and TV miniseries all around here." She glanced toward the breathtaking snowcapped Rockies in the distance. They looked as if they'd sprung up in the town's backyard. "Plus, the crews left behind a number of movie sets, and the town council is trying to decide how best to use them."

Ron gave her an annoying smirk.

With his dark hair and hazel eyes, Savannah had once considered him a good-looking man. He could also be charming when he wanted. Or he could be a first-class jerk.

"Are you going to just stand there?" The door remained slightly ajar, and when he didn't respond she considered giving it a push. He was a notorious hound dog. Putting him out of commission for a while would make many women in the office happy. How he'd managed to hold on to his job, she'd never know. "Move," she said, oh so tempted. "Please."

"What's it been, two years since you've been out in the field?" he said, finally stepping back. "Bet you're sorry you chose this assignment."

Ignoring him, she grabbed her purse and key fob and checked to make sure the car's license plate number was included in case the desk clerk asked for it.

"Ah, I get it," he said. "You wanted to get me alone."

"Yeah, that's right." She swung her legs out of the car and stood. In her heeled boots, she had an inch on him… which she liked. "How did *you* end up here?" At the last minute he'd replaced Duncan, who Savannah had requested to be part of the team. She never would've asked for Ron. "I thought you were headed to New Orleans."

"I pulled a few strings."

Frowning, she popped the trunk and went around to get her bags. "That doesn't make sense…"

Ron quickly lost the cocky grin and shrugged. "I wanted a shorter gig."

He looked as though he was holding something back, which made Savannah nervous. Of all the assignments, she couldn't have this one go sideways. He'd asked her out a couple times, and she'd politely declined. It had been a while, and everything had been fine between them, especially since she worked in the Denver office and he was usually on the road.

But God help him if he stuck one toe over the line. A nasty thought had her biting down on her lip. Wouldn't Ron just die if he knew she'd started seeing Porter Burke two months ago? She wouldn't say, of course, but just imagining the shock on his face brought her a moment's satisfaction.

He beat her to the bags, grabbing both of them.

"Thank you, Ron," she said, trying to keep her tone

pleasant. "But I've got it. You really should go catch up with Nina."

"Change of plans," he said, heading toward the motel entrance.

"What do you mean?" she asked, hurrying to keep up with him.

"I'm staying here, too."

"What? Wait. Duncan booked two rooms over at—"

"I changed the reservations."

"What do you mean you changed them? Without consulting me?"

They reached the door and he stepped back, exchanging a smile with an older woman exiting the building. It gave Savannah a minute to settle down and get her temper under control. She wanted to kill him, but instead she'd just maim him for life.

A couple was sorting through brochures in the lobby, which was small enough that it would be difficult for Savannah not to be overheard. A woman standing behind the front desk greeted them. Ron gave her a big smile, stepped up and set down the bags.

This was starting out just great. Ten crummy seconds. That was all Savannah would've needed to drag Ron back out to the parking lot without causing a scene.

"We're checking in," Ron said. "I believe you have our reservation. Mr. and Mrs. Ron Carver."

Savannah gaped at him, too stunned to say anything.

"Yes, we've been expecting you." The woman—Patty, according to her name tag—transferred her attention to a monitor screen. "Oh, and congratulations. I see you called this morning and requested a honeymoon suite—"

"What? No. That's a mistake." Savannah quietly cleared her throat as she tried to regain her wits. The woman looked confused. "We aren't really married. Not yet." Forcing a smile, Savannah elbowed Ron. "Quit being so impatient."

"Come on, honey. Don't be—"

"We need two rooms."

"Well, to be honest, we don't have anything like a honeymoon suite. But let's see what we do have…" Patty returned her gaze to the monitor. "How about a connecting—"

"No. Nothing connecting either." Savannah didn't trust herself to even look at Ron. "In fact, a different floor would be preferable."

"Savannah, honey…"

She pushed his arm away from her shoulders. "Actually, I'm still pretty upset with you from that last little stunt you pulled." The heel of her boot found his big toe. She didn't step down too hard.

Ron whimpered.

Oh, well maybe it was a tiny bit harder than she'd intended.

"I'm sorry, Patty." Savannah found it wasn't as difficult to smile this time. "I didn't mean to include you in our little tiff. Now, about my room?"

"No problem." The woman hid her amusement as well as Savannah hid her satisfaction over inflicting pain on the stupid bastard.

And she was in no way finished with him. Maiming was now officially off the table. Another cute move and she was going for the jugular.

She had to be careful, though. In their line of work, attracting too much attention sometimes ended with them giving themselves away. The town was a legitimate client paying for Porter Burke's services. The team had to give it their best effort.

Savannah hadn't once forgotten how much she had at stake here.

Life had been good to her these last six years. She had just about everything she could want and certainly more than she'd ever dreamed possible, given her background. But some elusive piece seemed to be missing, and she couldn't shake the feeling Blackfoot Falls might be the key.

The whole point of coming back to her childhood home was to get some closure. Being run out of town had been traumatic, and she'd had nightmares, plenty of them, for years. Now she'd see it all from an adult's perspective instead of a hormonal teen's.

This quest was one of completion, a symbolic way of locking the past behind her, so she could finally, unequivocally feel like the woman she appeared to be. Content, successful and capable of creating the life she wanted.

Now, if she could just figure out a way to get rid of Ron.

MIKE BURNETT SWUNG into the saddle and pulled up the collar of his jacket against the chilly October air. The sun had already dropped behind the snowcapped peaks to the west, so he didn't need to check the time to know he was running late. He'd hoped to be home well before sundown.

Maybe he was wrong about the calf straying this far. He thought he'd caught a glimpse of the little hellion in the brush, but it must've been a coyote.

After taking a final look around, he started down the ridge, scouring the overgrown sage while keeping Dude at a slow walk. As they approached the clearing, the gelding sniffed the air. His nostrils flaring, he danced impatiently, waiting for a signal.

Mike knew what was coming. "It's getting cold. Any chance I can talk you out of this?" he said, leaning forward and stroking the bay's neck. "Huh, you big baby?"

Dude decided that was permission enough and galloped toward the trees. They skirted a trio of pines, leaped over a fallen branch, raced past a grove of cottonwoods and then splashed across the creek. Mike could've done without that part of the ritual, but he'd had the bay for five years now and he liked that Dude still had the playfulness of a colt.

Besides, even in the cold, Mike still got a rush riding like the wind. He wasn't sure which one of them liked the exercise better.

After his own excitement leveled off, it was obvious Dude still needed to burn off some energy, and Mike didn't have the heart to slow him down. Together, they raced across the field, through the tall grass, until the barn came into view.

Chip, the part-timer he'd hired last spring, apparently hadn't left yet. His sorry old green pickup was still parked in the driveway. He was a good kid, still finding his way at the ripe old age of twenty-two, but he had a strong back and never complained about the work.

Right behind Chip's truck was a newer black crew cab that Mike didn't recognize. Course, there were about twenty trucks in the county that fit the same description.

Probably belonged to Victor or another friend of his parents who had come to see them before they left to spend the winter in Florida. For years they'd waited until after Thanksgiving to go stay with his sister, Lauren, and the grandkids and then returned by mid-April. But now all it took was the first dip in temperature to get them packing up their small trailer.

Mike wouldn't be surprised if they told him they were leaving Montana for good. His dad didn't need to be out in the cold dawn hours feeding the animals, what with his arthritis. Mike had taken over most of the chores, although his dad still managed to ride his old chestnut during the warmer months.

Chip walked out of the barn just as Mike rode up. "Hey,

your mom was looking for you." Chip glanced toward the house. "I think she wanted to catch you outside. I can take Dude."

"Thanks." Mike dismounted, wondering why the secrecy. "Whose truck?"

"Some old guy named Lawrence. I don't know him, but I seen him before…over by Twin Creeks."

"Ah." Mike had a bad feeling Lawrence was here to speak with him. "What are you still doing here? I figured you'd be at the Watering Hole by now."

Snorting, he took the reins. "I ain't setting foot in that place ever again. Those friggin' pool sharks from the Circle K hustled me out of fifty bucks and a round of beer."

"Never again, huh?"

Chip shrugged. "Or until next payday," he said, chuckling. "Gotta win my money back so I can buy my girl a ring. Hey, I heard you're pretty good."

"I don't know who told you that. I hold my own, but that's it."

"If you aren't doing anything tomorrow night, how about meeting me at the Full Moon? Maybe give me a few pointers? I'm buying."

Mike laughed. "You just said you were staying away from the game."

"Not from pool, just those Circle K crooks. And they stick to the Watering Hole."

Mike hadn't had a night out in a while. Probably do him some good. Especially with his folks gone. The house was going to be too quiet for the first few days. "Yeah, I just might do that. I'll even spring for the beer."

"Sweet." Chip tugged on the reins. "Come on, boy. I see he let you go swimming again."

Mike took off his Stetson and ran a hand through his hair as he turned toward the house. Before he could take another step, he heard the kitchen door squeak open. Time to oil the hinges again. The old log-and-stone house, which had been built by his granddad, needed some attention. Thankfully, Mike had the money to make the more urgent repairs over the slower winter months.

"Hey, Mom. Chip said you—"

She motioned for him to keep his voice down as she hurried toward him wearing her usual jeans and flannel shirt but no jacket. He was a good fifteen yards from the house and the windows were all shut tight. No one inside would overhear them. But he wasn't going to argue, if she'd even give him a second to get a word in.

At sixty-three years young and only five foot two, Rosemary Burnett was trim and energetic, and boy could she move when she put her mind to it. Probably didn't realize she was still wearing her fuzzy pink house slippers.

After a quick glance over her shoulder, she veered left and gestured for him to follow her to the barn.

They met just inside, out of view. "What's all the cloak-and-dagger about?"

"Lawrence Peabody is here," she said, her face flushed. "Okay."

"Claims he heard we're leaving in the morning and stopped to say goodbye. Now, when has that stingy old goat ever given your dad and me a second thought? Huh?"

Mike couldn't argue there.

"First thing out of his mouth was to ask where you were and what time you'd be back." She ducked her head to look past him toward the house. "If I were you, I'd climb right back on Dude and take off."

Mike smiled. The thought had occurred to him. "Maybe it's not what we think."

"Of course it is, Michael. Didn't you hear? He's expanding his sundry store over in Twin Creeks, and there's talk he's buying the old drive-through in Blackfoot Falls and making it into a restaurant. I bet you dollars to doughnuts he wants you to do carpentry work for him."

"If he asks, I'll explain I'm too busy."

She reached up and cradled his left cheek with a motherly hand. "Will you, honey?"

"Winter might be a slow time, but I've got a lot of repairs to make around the house and barn."

"I understand why it's hard for you to say no to some of these folks. Lord knows what we would've done without the money you brought in during those lean years. Most folks could've waited to get their repairs done, but they called out of the kindness of their hearts. We both know Lawrence Peabody wasn't one of them."

"I haven't forgotten." He meant it. Mike felt no obligation to the man who had taken advantage of the Burnetts' situation.

Like most everyone in the ranching community, Mike and his family had struggled for a while. The recession had hit the whole country hard. But friends and neighbors had really stepped up, hiring him to do anything from minor repairs to remodeling work on kitchens.

Only one person had haggled him down to a ridiculously low price: Lawrence Peabody. So, no, Mike wasn't about to do any more work for the man.

Ultimately the family and the ranch had survived, and they were doing well now. They'd increased the herd to seven hundred head, which kept him damn busy. In fact, he'd decided to talk to his dad about offering Chip full-time work. They could afford it now and still be able to hire seasonal help.

"Well, I'd better hurry back inside before Lawrence catches on that I warned you." She started to leave, noticed her house slippers and sighed. "I'll chase him out in a bit. We still have some packing to do."

"No need to do anything on my account. I have no problem telling him no. What time are you leaving tomorrow?"

"Before the rooster crows. You know your father." She took a few steps and stopped. "I'm sorry we're leaving you here alone for Thanksgiving, Michael. I really—"

"Don't give it another thought. The cold is getting harder on Dad. I'm glad you're leaving now." It seemed like the perfect time to ask if she thought they might do better living in a warmer climate. But the sad smile that lifted the corners of her mouth stopped him.

"You should come to Florida for Christmas. Your sister and the kids miss you. Little Jared is getting so big, you won't believe it when you see him."

"Well, I've got fences to mend before I can even get to the house repairs—"

"It's not fair, son." She blinked, tears bringing a sheen to her eyes. "So much of the burden has rested on your shoulders. But I don't know what to do about it."

"Come on, Mom." He put an arm around her, aware that he'd just gotten his answer. "I wouldn't want to be anyplace else but right here. I love ranching, you know that."

"Good thing. I'm just plain too old to have more sons," she said with that wry sense of humor they shared.

Mike laughed. "Look, about Florida, we'll see. I just might surprise you."

"Better yet, I wish you'd find a girl," she said. "A nice young woman who understands what it means to live on a ranch and work outside come rain or shine." She squinted at him. "Oh, don't you give me that look. I know you want that, too."

He didn't bother to deny it. Now that things had settled

back to normal and he could actually make a decent living, he figured it was time to find the right woman. Didn't mean he'd hold his breath, though.

Chapter Two

The Full Moon Saloon looked like the place to be. Only seven thirty on a weeknight and it was hopping. Mostly locals, from what Savannah could tell as she and Ron searched for a table.

Nina was already sitting at the bar and being chatted up by a cowboy. She didn't look too put out by the attention, or by the loud jukebox blaring country music several feet from her. Though if it drowned Ron out, Savannah wouldn't complain. They'd been in town only one day, and she'd had it with him. Maybe it was time for them to have a big public argument so she could call off the engagement. Send him back to Denver without anyone at the motel getting too nosy.

Just thinking of the possibility was enough to cheer her up. In fact, she'd misjudged the scope of the job. They'd never had a small town client before, and it really didn't require three people. He'd claimed he wanted a shorter assignment. Maybe she could find a way to justify sending him back early.

The place hadn't grown much. To an isolated teenage girl, Blackfoot Falls had seemed much bigger and more exciting. And maybe it had shone a little brighter years ago. But so many shops on Main Street had closed during the economic crunch. The mayor wanted to give reluctant would-be shop owners a little boost, convince them it was time to take another chance.

"Check it out," Ron said, nodding at the stage and dance floor. "I wonder if they do the hokey pokey here. I bet they give lessons."

"Don't be an ass," she muttered and then hurried to a table that had just been vacated.

She took the seat that gave her a good view of the bar and then kicked the leg of the other chair so Ron wouldn't sit too close to her. Of course, he just dragged it closer.

"Sit across from me," she said, just as the waitress squeezed through behind him. "You're in the way."

"We're supposed to be engaged."

Savannah glared at him, even though the woman probably hadn't paid any attention at all. "You need to watch it."

"Oh, I am." Grinning, he slid his arm along the back of her chair. "I like that blouse. Did you wear it for me?"

So annoyed with him that she'd forgotten what she was wearing, she glanced down at the silky denim-like shirt. A gap offered a small peek of her pink bra. Sighing, she adjusted it, using the opportunity to dig her elbow into Ron's ribs.

He just laughed. "Shouldn't we be holding hands and making out or something?"

"Yeah, why don't you try it?"

"What's up with you, anyway?" He leaned back to look at her. "Every single woman in the office would go out with me in a minute. But not you, Miss High-and-Mighty."

Unbelievable. "Why haven't you gotten fired yet?" Savannah studied him. "That's not a rhetorical question. I honestly want to know how you've managed to keep your job."

"The clients love me."

"Maybe," she said grudgingly. "But don't be so sure about the women in the office."

His frown of disbelief was cut short when his phone signaled a text. Fine with her. She checked her own phone then scooted her chair several inches over and glanced around.

A few cowboys were playing pool in the back and trying to impress a group of women she guessed were from the Sundance dude ranch. She'd learned all about the place while getting a mani-pedi at the Cut and Curl earlier that day. Which was exactly what she'd hoped for. Even though she'd done her research and the mayor had given her a rundown, nothing beat the local beauty shop for getting the real feel of a town.

It had surprised Savannah that the McAllister family, who owned the Sundance, had gone the dude ranch route, since they were in the business of raising cattle. But the new venture had been wildly successful. So another ranch owner had followed their lead, while two smaller operations were thinking of opening B & Bs.

The waitress stopped at the table just as Ron put his phone away. "Sorry, folks. Hope you haven't waited too long," the brunette said with a friendly smile. "What can I get you?"

"Do you have champagne?"

"Oh, God, Ron, would you—" Savannah cut herself short when the woman glanced at her.

"Well, excuse me for wanting to toast my bride-to-be." Ron shrugged, looking to the waitress for sympathy.

"Oh, that's so sweet," she said. "I'm sorry, we don't have champagne. We do carry a couple of decent wines, though."

"You're right. That was very sweet." Savannah forced a smile and touched Ron's hand. "I'll take a beer. Whatever you have on tap."

The woman nodded and looked at Ron.

"Be right back," Savannah said, withdrawing her hand and making a break for it before he could say anything.

She dug several bills out of her jeans pocket to get some change then leaned on the bar near the jukebox while she waited for the bartender to finish pouring a line of shots. Another hour with Ron and she was going to be ordering some of that tequila herself.

Nina was two bar stools away, still laughing it up with the long-haired cowboy. When she noticed Savannah, she said something to the guy, and he disappeared. Left his mug of beer, though, so he couldn't have gone too far.

When Nina gave her a questioning look, Savannah realized her mistake. She'd only wanted to get away from Ron and to browse the jukebox selections. Hopefully find something that wasn't country. But now Nina thought Savannah was trying to get her attention.

The bartender glanced over at her. "Be with you in a minute," she called out from halfway down the bar.

"Take your time," Savannah replied. "And I mean that with all my heart." She smiled at Nina. "My fiancé is driving me nuts. So I'm ditching him for a while."

"Ah." Nina dialed down her grin. "Well, if you're only at the engagement stage, there's still time."

"Don't I wish."

"My heart goes out to you."

"Thanks." Savannah laughed and peered down the row of customers sitting on the stools. Mostly cowboys in their twenties and thirties. Nobody she recognized, but she really didn't expect to see anyone she would remember. Or who would remember her.

Earlier, at the diner, she'd bumped into an older woman who looked familiar, and that had put Savannah on edge. But it was just nerves, which she suspected had more to do with Ron and how he seemed to be shadowing her every move.

"Are you visiting?" Nina asked, just as the bartender was approaching.

Savannah nodded. "You?"

"Yep. I'm from Nebraska. On my way to Glacier National Park."

"Traveling alone?" Savannah asked conversationally.

"Yep."

The bartender smiled at Savannah. "What can I get you?"

"Change for the jukebox, please."

"You got it." She opened the register and glanced at the dollar bills Savannah laid on the counter before she started digging out quarters. "Couldn't help overhearing," she said. "For what it's worth, men outnumber women two to one in this county."

"Wow." Nina's eyes lit up. "Good to know."

"Yeah, lucky you. Hey, my fiancé is pretty good-looking," Savannah said, as the bartender dropped the coins in her palm. "I'll trade you."

Both women grinned.

A waitress called out, "Mallory," and the blonde bartender gave her a nod. "You guys need anything else, let me know," she said, slapping the bar before heading off.

"You knew that, didn't you?" Savannah murmured. "That's why you stuck me with Ron."

Nina laughed. "Nope. That switch was all his idea."

Savannah sighed. Even so, Nina should've cleared it with her first. "I'd better get back before he comes over and bothers me."

She swung around and ran right into a wall of hard, solid male. Her breath left her in a whoosh, and she stumbled back against the bar with a fair amount of force.

A hand shot out to steady her. "I'm sorry, ma'am. Are you okay?"

"Fine." She brushed the hair away from her warm cheeks. The bar had to be made of solid oak. She'd hit it at an odd angle, and it would probably leave a bruise, but she was more embarrassed than anything else.

"Did I hurt you?" He eased his grip on her arm and lowered his hand.

"It wasn't your fault, it was mine." She finally looked up at his face. Classically handsome. Dark hair, cut short. Dark eyes. Tall...

Oh, God. She knew him.

Mike something. His family had owned a ranch about three miles from where she'd lived in that run-down cabin. They hadn't actually spoken...he was older, but he'd always waved when he saw her walking to the creek, where she used to hide out, anxious to get away from her parents' endless arguments until her dad had finally left.

One time, Mike had even offered her a ride in his truck. Savannah had always had a book with her. That day, though, she'd been carrying three heavy hardbacks and enough snacks to last her a week. Just in case she had gotten brave enough to run away. It was the only time she'd seen him up close. She remembered because she'd thought he had kind eyes.

Burnett. That was his last name.

Nina touched her arm. "Are you okay?" she asked, clearly concerned.

"What?" Savannah blinked at her. "Yes, I'm fine." Her gaze went back to Mike. "How about you?"

His mouth quirked up a little at the corners. "Right as rain."

"Good. Okay." She swallowed at the way he was staring at her. Didn't mean he recognized her. He probably just thought she was some crazy woman. "Again, I'm so sorry," she said, stepping around him and then hurrying to the table.

"What the hell was that about?" Ron asked.

"Nothing. I wasn't paying attention and plowed into that guy."

Ron frowned. "So why were you staring at each other?"

"I—I don't know. I was in shock." She touched her side, which barely hurt. "Plus I think I bruised my ribs."

"Want me to have a look?"

"Gee, how kind of you to offer." She turned away from his boorish grin. And sneaked another peek at Mike.

He picked up a mug of beer the bartender had just slid over to him and then carried it into the back room. Even if Savannah hadn't seen him up close, she would've recognized his loose, easy stride. It was pretty amazing, the things that had stuck with her. The smell of the first day at the public school. The sound of the creek near the cabin. The way the kids had stared at her that awful day. And the kindness of her neighbor.

"Did you hear me?"

Savannah had vaguely heard him say something about Kalispell. "What about it?" she said, starting to pick up the beer the waitress had left. Only then did she realize she was still clutching the handful of quarters. "Oh, damn. I forgot to choose some songs."

Her heart picked up speed. From here she couldn't see Mike. But from the jukebox she'd have a great view of the back room. The thought worried her. If anything, she should be staying clear of him. Just in case...

"Come on, you don't really want to stick around. There's gotta be a lot more happening in Kalispell than this hick town."

"But their mayor didn't hire us, did he?" She should've

lowered her voice. "You know what? You're right." She reached into her jeans pocket and pulled out the rental key. "Go. Have a good time. I'll team up with Nina."

"Ah, you're anxious to get rid of me." He took the keys, raising his right eyebrow at her. "So you two can pick up all the cowboys you want."

"Don't be an idiot."

Ron glanced toward the back room. "We're supposed to be the happily engaged couple," he said, returning his arm to the back of her chair and leaning close. "What would people think?"

"Okay, I was wrong about the town and our approach. Is that what you wanted to hear? We don't need to see how they roll out the carpet for a special occasion. This isn't that kind of getaway. So feel free to hit Kalispell. On the company's dime." At this point, Savannah would gladly pay his expenses out of her own pocket. "Stay a few days, write up something that relates to Blackfoot Falls and I'll take care of it from there."

Ron studied her for a long, unnerving moment. "Nah, I kind of like this arrangement," he said, tightening his arm around her.

It took all of her willpower not to react. "Maybe you should go back to Denver. I'm sure there's another assignment better suited to your taste."

He shook his head. "Hicksville is starting to grow on me."

Savannah reared back when it looked as if he might try to kiss her. "Don't you dare. And if I hear *Hicksville* one more time, you are going back to Denver whether you like it or not."

His mouth curved in a cocky smile. "Don't let that supervisor title go to your head. The only reason I haven't moved up the chain is because I don't want the headache."

She wondered if he resented her promotion—the one she'd worked hard for and totally deserved. "You're being unprofessional. I don't care if you think this job doesn't matter or that no one will pay attention to your snide remarks. In a place like this? Everyone knows everything, and what they aren't quite sure of, they'll fill in with information that will fuel the best gossip. No matter who they harm or what they—" She stopped and took a breath when she saw how oddly he was looking at her. "Anyway, we don't need our impression tainted or our recommendations not taken seriously."

"That's some insight," he said in a slightly mocking tone. "How do you know so much about it? Where are you from?"

She rolled her eyes. "Everyone knows how small towns operate." She picked up her mug before she mouthed off again.

As she took a sip, she saw Mike emerge from the back room, his gaze sweeping the bar and briefly lingering on her before he turned away.

Her stomach did a complete somersault.

Chapter Three

Mike set his beer on the bar and smiled at the dark-haired woman sitting two stools away and eyeing him as he waited for Mallory. She didn't look familiar, but the woman who'd bumped into him earlier sure did.

"Hey, it's good to see you, Mike," Mallory said as she walked up. "Sorry I couldn't talk before. It's been a while, hasn't it?"

"Yep, been busy. So have you, I see."

"Business is great. I'm only closed one day a week now. And that's just for the sake of my sanity."

"Glad to hear it." Mike had gotten to know her a little when he'd done some carpentry work for her. He'd already quit doing side jobs by the time she'd moved to town, but he couldn't say no. Frankly, had she been available, he would've asked her out. "Listen, the woman I almost ran over earlier, do you know her?"

Mallory glanced past him and shook her head. "I've never seen her before. Probably a tourist. She's sitting with a guy, though."

Mike smiled. "I was just curious. She looked familiar, but I couldn't place her."

"Ah." She stared past him again. "Well, for what it's worth, she might be sitting with the dude, but I'm guessing she's not thrilled about it."

Mike choked out a laugh. "Thanks. I'll pass." Picking up his mug, he stepped back, remembered what happened before and checked to see if he was clear.

The woman on the bar stool smiled. "What's going on back there?" she asked with a glance toward the pool tables. "Anything interesting?"

"Besides pool, there's darts and a mechanical bull."

"Sounds fun."

He looked at Mallory, who hadn't strayed far and was wiping the counter. "Is the bull working?"

"Should be."

The woman laughed. "I meant the pool. The bull...not so much."

"If you want to play, you won't have any trouble finding someone to go up against." He hoped that didn't sound like a brush-off, even though it was.

"I'm waiting for someone," she said with a small shrug. "Maybe later."

Mallory dropped the rag as Mike turned to leave. "Want another beer to take back with you?"

"Nah," he said, holding up the half-full mug. "This should do me. I gotta get up early tomorrow."

"Well, don't be a stranger. Winter should slow you down some at the ranch."

"You're right." Mike fought the urge to glance over at the blonde before he disappeared into the back. It wasn't just that she was attractive. It was driving him nuts not being able to place her. But it was also obvious she wasn't from Blackfoot Falls or anywhere nearby. She was most definitely a city woman. So not much chance he knew her at all.

Ah, hell.

He sneaked a look.

And damned if she wasn't looking right back at him.

Trouble was, she wasn't just sitting with the guy. They

were so close to each other a stiff breeze couldn't slip between them. Mallory was right, though. The woman didn't look all that happy with the setup.

He headed back to the pool tables. Chip stood in the corner chalking his cue and frowning. "I was wondering where you were," he said. "We're up next."

Mike set his beer down next to Chip's mug on the ledge then picked up his own cue. "I haven't played in a couple of years so don't expect much."

"Bet you're still better than me." Snorting, Chip downed half his beer in one pull.

"You drink like that when you play the Circle K boys?"

Chip's sheepish expression was his answer. "How's your pitching arm these days?"

"My what?"

"I heard about you," Chip said. "You played ball in high school and in college, too. I ran into Kenny Edwards at the pawnshop the other day. When I told him I was working for you, he said he used to be your high-school coach."

"That was a long time ago." Mike watched a lanky young guy in a camo T-shirt sink two stripes on the break. His cocky grin wasn't doing him any favors. Another tip for Chip—don't get cocky, especially when booze is involved.

"Kenny said you should've gone pro. You were that good."

"Yeah, well, Kenny's wrong."

"Wait," Chip said. "Weren't you scouted for a farm team? I can't see Kenny lying about something like that."

The other table had only four balls plus the eight ball left, and the two guys from the Lone Wolf seemed evenly matched. He and Chip would be up in a couple minutes. Sooner if the guys would quit showing off for the three women cooing words of encouragement.

They had to be tourists, sipping their fancy drinks and

flirting shamelessly. Mike couldn't listen to them or talk about baseball without thinking of Ellen. He'd known his ex-wife most of his life. Or at least, he thought he had. They'd married the summer after graduating from college. Turned out, though, being married to a professional ballplayer was more important to Ellen than being married to him.

"So? Did Kenny exaggerate?"

"No," Mike said finally. "I could've played for the Billings Mustangs. Just like a whole lot of other guys." In his heart, he'd known he didn't have what it took to play pro ball. And it wasn't as if he didn't like ranching. Hell, it was in his blood.

Chip's thick brows lowered into a frown. "A *lot* of guys? I don't think so."

"They're only a farm team."

"Yeah, for the Cincinnati Reds. Do you know how many major-league heavy hitters came out of farm teams? Most of 'em, probably."

"Why are you bringing this up? It's all history. You should be watching these guys and learning a few tricks." Mike nodded at the kid in the camo T-shirt. "He'll need to use inside English on this shot. If he does it well, the ball will curve right into the hole."

After the shot—perfectly executed—he realized Chip was back to staring at him.

"You know," Chip said, a hopeful gleam in his eyes. "Sometimes the Circle K guys play softball. How about if you—"

"Not interested." Mike shook his head.

"Why not? Those guys are all young, probably about my age. They wouldn't know about you playing baseball back in the day."

Mike couldn't help but laugh. "Yeah, maybe you shouldn't imply I'm old if you want a favor."

"So, you are thinking about it?"

"Softball isn't even the same—" Mike saw the blonde walk up to the jukebox and completely forgot what he was going to say.

SAVANNAH SCANNED THE long list of songs. She hadn't heard of most of them, but then she'd always been horrible at remembering titles. Or even knowing what they were in the first place. And frankly, she didn't have time to listen to music. Work managed to eat up most of the hours in her day. During her commute to and from the office, she generally listened to self-help CDs. After all, no matter how much she loved her life and career, there was always room for improvement.

"Hey."

Startled by Nina's voice practically in her ear, Savannah turned on her with a glare. "What are you doing? We can't suddenly be best friends."

Nina gave her a funny look. "Jesus, you've been riding a desk too long. You really need to chill."

Savannah supposed she might be letting paranoia mess with her head and then, worse, overreacting. "What is it?"

"That cowboy from earlier… I think the bartender called him Mike? He was asking her about you."

Savannah's heart nearly exploded. "Asking about what?"

"He wanted to know if she'd seen you before. Said he thought you looked familiar."

Savannah leaned on the jukebox for support. This was bad. So, so bad.

"Obviously it was just a line," Nina said, glancing over the song selection. "Oh, and he's hot and I hate you."

"Duly noted." Somehow, Savannah managed to stay calm. "Why don't you go after him?"

"I tried. He wasn't interested." She shrugged. "Anyway, I didn't want to say anything in front of Ron. But if I were you, I'd totally ditch his ass and go for the cowboy."

They both laughed, and Savannah relaxed. Maybe Nina was right and it was just a line. The possibility that he could actually be attracted to her sent a little shiver down her spine.

But wait…he wouldn't need to use a *line* with the bartender. Savannah circled back to worrying. Still, how could he remember a girl he'd never really known or had ever seen more than a dozen times from afar? *Fourteen years ago?*

Nina pointed to something on the jukebox. Savannah squinted to see what it was then realized Nina was covering up the fact that they'd lingered too long and for no apparent reason. No one was paying them any attention, but she'd get the third degree from Ron.

"I'd better scoot," Nina whispered. Then in a louder voice as she backed away she said, "Thanks for letting me cut in with my song."

"No problem." Savannah shot a quick look in Ron's direction before returning to the song list. He was still answering texts.

She'd chosen several songs, but she couldn't for the life of her recall what they were. What she really wanted to do was check out the back room, but she knew she'd better wait until Mike left.

It was a tough call. Should she get it over with, see if he remembered her? Or try to avoid him? She wondered how often he came into town. All she really had to do was stay away from the two bars. Maybe the diner and steak house, too. And probably the Food Mart and variety store just to be safe. Definitely the hardware store but that one was easy.

Oh, hell. The town wasn't all that big. Twenty-three hundred people in the whole county, most of them spread out on ranches and farms.

Should she or shouldn't she?

Since she couldn't decide, she figured the smart thing would be to leave. Ron had had one foot out the door from the minute they'd arrived. If she pleaded a headache and went to her room, he just might decide to hit Kalispell.

And she'd be left in peace to write up today's notes. If she were to run into Mike again, at least she'd be more prepared.

Taking a step backward, she was struck with the temptation to steal a quick look at the pool players. All she had to do was turn her head to the right…just for a second…

She moved back another step and felt something directly behind her.

A deep rumbling laugh caressed her ears.

"We've gotta stop doing this." It was Mike's voice. His laugh. His hand touching her lower back.

Savannah whirled around.

He stood a couple feet away, holding his almost-empty mug aloft. Enough beer remained to have made a collision unpleasantly wet.

"Sorry, sorry, I didn't look. Again." She glanced helplessly at Nina, who arched a brow at her, clearly trying not to laugh.

"Excuse me," another voice said from behind her. "Could I squeeze by to get to the jukebox?"

Savannah turned, and as she moved out of the way, smiled an apology at the woman trying to hold on to a fistful of quarters. When she switched her gaze to Mike, the intensity with which he was studying her jolted her back to the problem.

If she wanted to test the waters, now was the time.

But Nina was right there, not more than ten feet away now. And Ron...he could be charging toward them for all she knew.

Savannah turned her head and saw that he was still pre-occupied with his phone. She inched around so that she wasn't directly facing Nina.

"I'm usually not this oblivious," she said, keeping her voice low and steady, even as her courage faltered. "I would really appreciate it if you'd let me pay for a refill."

"I didn't spill a drop," he said with an easy smile. "But if you have the time, I'd like to buy you a drink."

"Oh. No." Her mouth went dry. "All I meant... I'd just—" She cleared her throat. "I'm with someone." She glanced briefly toward Ron. "But I'd like to pay for your beer. You know, as an apology. That's what I meant..."

His smile faded. "I understand," he said, nodding slowly. "Can I ask you a quick question?"

This was it.

Savannah was an idiot. She wasn't prepared, and there was nothing she could do but listen. "Okay."

"Have we met before?"

Her chest actually hurt, though she didn't think it was anything serious. Yeah, why would she get off that easily? "No," she said, and even managed a smile. "I don't see how."

"You're not from around here?"

"Nope."

"Billings?"

She shook her head. "Denver."

"It's not a line. You really do look familiar."

She shrugged. "I get that a lot."

Mike frowned. "I can't see why," he said, his whiskey-brown gaze roaming over her face and lingering briefly on her mouth. "I'm Mike, by the way."

"Savannah." She'd gone by Elizabeth back then, if he'd known her name at all. Her middle name should throw him. "Well, I'd better get back to the table. I promise not to bulldoze over you again."

"No worries. I'm tough," he said with a dazzling smile. It disappeared in the next instant. "I know where I've seen you—you were that kid—" He cut himself short and, with a slight frown, searched her eyes.

Panic roiled in her stomach. She heard a whimper and, with a start, realized it had come from her. Unable to move, she stayed frozen in her tracks as she silently pleaded with him to not give her away.

"No," he said after the longest ten seconds on record. "I was thinking of someone I met at the Denver stockyards a while back." He moved to let someone pass. "Ever been there?"

She just shook her head.

"Sorry, my mistake." With a quick smile, he shrugged and walked away.

Chapter Four

Savannah had slept in longer than she'd intended, so by the time she hit the continental breakfast in the lobby, the only thing left on the silver trays was a blueberry muffin and some kind of fruit Danish bearing the indent of someone's finger.

Good thing she wasn't all that hungry. She could smell the coffee, though. Before she made it to the cart with the silver urn, a woman came out from a room behind the desk.

"Looking for coffee?" she asked, and Savannah nodded. "I was just coming to check if I needed to make a fresh pot."

"I'll let you know in a second."

"I'll go on and get some started. It seems you got short-changed," the woman said, nodding at the table.

"I'm late." Savannah grabbed a cup. "My fault, not yours." She flipped the lever and watched the dark sludgy brew stream into the cup.

"Oh, for heaven's sake, I promise it'll just take a minute." The older woman's updo was a '60s-style beehive like the one Savannah had seen in pictures of her late grandmother. Glancing at the bowl of apples, the woman hustled back around the desk then paused at the door. "I have some oranges, if you're interested."

"Thanks, but I think I'll go see what they have at the bakery."

"Well, I feel just terrible. You paid for a room same as everyone else. We should feed you breakfast."

Savannah smiled. "Actually, I'm going over there for a latte. So, please, don't worry about it."

The woman darted a look at the glass door. "You know, your fiancé left about ten minutes ago. Maybe he went to get something to surprise you."

Savannah frowned. She'd only spoken with Patty at the desk, and yet this woman knew Ron was her fiancé. Oh, great.

"We haven't met. I'm Maxine." She pointed to her name tag. "It's Patty's day off. She told me you had a handsome fiancé, and my word she didn't do him justice at all. You're very lucky," she whispered, nodding sagely.

Savannah dug up a smile. "Yep, he's a peach, all right." She scanned what she could see of the parking lot. "Any chance you saw which way he went?"

"Hmm, well, he got in his car…"

Of course…he still had her key. "Okay, thanks, Maxine."

"I'll have fresh-made before you get back, hon."

Savannah kept walking but waved an acknowledgment. As soon as she was outside, she remembered she needed money and glanced around as she patted the pockets of her jeans. Luckily, she found a crumpled five-dollar bill and some change.

Crossing the parking lot at a clip, Savannah headed toward the bakery. Two shops down was the steak house that had reopened in the last year. Halfway there, she felt the chill seeping in through the lightweight sweatshirt she'd thrown on just to grab coffee in the lobby. It was in no way adequate for a chilly fall morning.

They had quite a full schedule today. Nina had obtained a list of people who were turning portions of their ranches or bunkhouses into guest quarters, mostly in line with a B & B

rather than a dude ranch. Savannah figured they could form
a co-op in order to offer the same kind of activities that actual dude ranches provided. But she'd know more after she'd
visited with them.

The brisk walk helped wake her up, but she was more
than ready for a hazelnut latte by the time she opened the
door to The Cake Whisperer. What she wasn't ready for
was a crowd. It seemed half the population of Blackfoot
Falls had squeezed into the small bakery. The benches on
the right were taken, as were the only two chairs. Standing a little too close together were dusty cowboys, a couple
young moms, several older ladies…

…and Mike.

Wearing a Stetson, the brim pulled low, he stood off to
the side, his head bowed toward an older woman as he listened to whatever she was telling him.

What on earth was he doing in town this early? Shouldn't
he be feeding horses or milking cows or something?

Savannah seriously thought about slipping back out.
And she didn't much care if he noticed.

"Oh, don't be shy, honey." A tiny white-haired lady
caught Savannah's arm with a surprising grip. "Not everyone's in line. They're just gossiping. You just step right
on up here," she said, tugging on Savannah.

"Thanks, but I think I'll come back later."

The door opened behind her, and three women crammed
into the shop. They kept chatting, apparently unaware that
they were literally breathing down the back of her neck.

"Is there a special on today?" Savannah muttered.

The white-haired lady chuckled. "Kylie," she said, nodding at the woman reaching into the display case. "She's
the owner. She bought a fancy coffee machine, and now
she's got a bunch of us hooked on caramel lattes. Ever
heard of them?"

"Um, actually, yes." Between the scent of the coffee and the fresh-baked aroma of cinnamon and sugar, her stomach wasn't all that pleased about leaving and let her know it. She risked a glance at Mike.

He was looking right at her.

Savannah sighed. On top of really not wanting to engage with him, she probably looked like crap, since she hadn't intended to go beyond the motel lobby.

It wasn't too late to make a getaway.

"Excuse me," she said, pulling back her arm. "I really don't have time to wait."

The woman blinked. "Aren't you visiting?"

"Yes," she said, glancing over her shoulder so she wouldn't run someone over. That hadn't gone so well last night.

"Well, honey, you shouldn't be in such a hurry. I'm Eunice. What's your name?"

"Savannah, but I'm not on vacation. And honestly, I don't mean to be rude…" she said, inching backward.

The door opened again just as a young girl slipped past her to leave. One customer down as two more entered.

A big, burly cowboy nodded at her. His younger sidekick just stared, his cheeks turning a little pink when someone jostled her and she pressed against him.

"Okay, everyone, this is ridiculous." The owner had straightened and was surveying the crowd while another woman operated the espresso machine, not once looking up. "Anyone who's already gotten their order, please step outside and give everyone else room."

"It's chilly out there," came a voice from the front.

"You need to expand, Kylie," someone else said.

"I'm working on it." She handed over a white box and some change. "In the meantime, I don't want to get fined for having too many customers in here."

"Who's gonna do that? Grace?"

"Yes, Grace or one of her deputies. There are fire laws about occupancy, and I'm over the limit. So, please…"

Savannah would be happy to comply if they'd let her through. "Excuse me," she said to the two men, motioning with her hand for them to give her a clear path.

"Okay, everyone." Mike's voice rose above the murmurs. Except he wasn't standing off to the side anymore. He'd moved closer to her. "Kylie's right. This isn't safe. And it's not fair to people who haven't been waited on yet. So, come on…it's not going to kill anyone to step outside."

After a chorus of grumbling, people started to move toward the door. Savannah made it onto the sidewalk. But she'd barely had time for a sigh of relief when Mike appeared next to her.

"Hey, it shouldn't be a long wait," he said. "Some folks just want a doughnut."

"What are you doing here?" she asked. "Don't you have hogs to slop? Feed to pitch? Cows to milk?"

He choked out a laugh. "I think you have me confused with someone else."

"Well, aren't those the kind of things people do on ranches?"

"Some, I suppose. Assuming they have milk cows and hogs."

"Oh. Right," she said, backing away and feeling like a complete dope. "Well, nice seeing you again."

"Hey, look, I just wanted to say that if I made you uncomfortable last night, I'm sorry."

"No, no," she said. "It's totally fine. You mistook me for someone else. We've all done that at one time or another…"

His brows drew together. Something in his expression began to chip away at her confidence. She'd hoped he hadn't recognized her for certain, but maybe she hadn't fooled him.

Was he expecting her to come clean? Confess that she was, in fact, Elizabeth Savannah Riley? She was Savannah James now. She'd legally changed her last name to her mom and stepfather's when she was sixteen.

She shouldn't worry he'd say anything untoward though. He'd certainly been discreet last night. "I'm sorry, I'm just… I have a lot to do today." She looked behind her then took another step back.

"Right. Sightseeing."

She smiled and nodded.

"You should go have a look at the creek. It's risen in the last couple of years, with the heavy winters."

Her stomach lurched. Did he mean *her* creek? The one where she'd spent half her childhood? He hadn't been specific. More evidence he knew exactly who she was?

"I'll see you soon, I'm sure," she said, then turned, refraining from darting across the street so it wouldn't seem as if she was running from him. Even though he couldn't think anything else.

Why on earth had she put herself in this situation? Everything could blow up in her face, and it would be her own fault. Why had she thought it would be quick and simple to slip in and out of town and put the old haunting memories to bed for good, without anyone being the wiser?

Now she had to depend on Mike not outing her. He'd already proved himself, but her ditching him like a bad date might turn that around, and then where would she be?

This was the perfect time to figure out how deep a hole she'd dug for herself. Do some damage control. She wouldn't dare acknowledge Mike when she was with Ron or Nina. They'd want an explanation that could cost her dearly. Worse, it could cost the company this job and damage its reputation.

Savannah turned around and headed back to the bakery, hoping he was still there. A gray truck was coming toward her. As it got closer, she saw Mike behind the wheel. He slowed down and lowered the passenger-side window.

"Can I offer you a lift?" he asked, despite the fact they were now headed in opposite directions.

"No thanks," she said, but she found herself hopping in anyway. Guess she needed a bit more calm.

He rubbed his jaw and laughed.

"I know. Ignore me," she said, and managed a slight smile. "We need to talk."

He drove a short way then pulled over to the curb. "Okay. Shoot. I assume this has something to do with your fiancé?"

Her face got hot, and it was hard to look at Mike without blurting out every last thing. Of course he knew about Ron. He'd known it last night. "That's not the only thing," she said, then worked up the nerve to meet his eyes. "I don't want anyone to know who I am. I'm frankly shocked you recognized me. It was so long ago."

"I'll admit, you've changed. I wasn't sure at first."

"You were very kind last night. I didn't even realize how kind until this morning. I appreciate it. And honestly, I'd like to explain why I'm here, but it's kind of complicated."

"Hey, it's nobody's business why you're here, including mine," he said, shrugging. "Don't worry, I won't say anything."

He wouldn't. She knew it. Even though curiosity was alive in his gaze. It was so tempting to spill it all. To let him know that Ron wasn't her fiancé, far from it. Mike had to remember exactly what had chased her and her mom out of town. She'd had so few interactions with the people in Blackfoot Falls—a rare lunch at the diner, some trips to the market and then getting to attend school, which had seemed like a miracle but had ended up a public disaster. Mike had always been nice, though.

It would feel good to explain why she was here, that it was for her job. That she'd overcome her unfortunate past and made something of herself.

"Savannah?"

What was she thinking? She couldn't admit any of that. Not yet. After she gave the presentation, then maybe. In the meantime, she needed to keep her head down, stay focused on the job. And not be sitting in his truck for everyone to see. Jeez. Talk about stirring the pot. She glanced around and noticed her rental heading their way, with Ron driving it.

She ducked down, bumping her forehead on the dashboard. "Drive. Please. Anywhere but the motel parking lot."

Mike didn't say a word, just put the truck in gear and zoomed out of there. He turned the corner, made another turn, drove some more then turned again. If he kept that up, it wouldn't just be butterflies she was feeling.

Finally, he said, "I think we're in the clear."

When she poked her head up, she saw he'd pulled into a vacant lot behind the motel. "Okay. This is good," she said, checking the side mirror. They were at the edge of town; the only thing past the motel was a gas station. "I'm sorry about that. About everything. But thank you."

Before he had a chance to speak, she opened the door and jumped out.

"Wait."

She considered ignoring him. But she didn't want to make things worse and not just because he could cause problems. It wasn't fair to him.

After another cautious look around, she got back in but left the door ajar. "There is an explanation," she said, keeping her voice level. "I promise. Trust me, if you can. For a bit."

"I meant it, Savannah, it's none of my business."

"I know," she said. "I'd actually like to tell you as soon as I'm at liberty to do so."

Now he looked twice as curious. "Look, I hope this isn't out of line, but I'm glad I got to see you. You were such a shy kid, I couldn't help wondering what had happened to you." His smile filled the cab with its warmth. "You've come a long way. You should be very proud of yourself."

His words brought a lump to her throat. She hadn't realized just how much she needed to hear that. Barely able to swallow, she said, "Thank you, Mike. I don't… I should go."

She jumped out before he could say anything else. Or she ended up oversharing. The emotion he'd tapped into ran deep, so deep she wondered what else was buried down there.

But now wasn't the time to start digging for insight. She saw an entrance next to a loading dock and figured it was for employees. The brisk walk and morning chill felt good as she skirted the building to get to the front entrance. Dying for some coffee and time to get back her sense of control, she forgot to check the lot for Ron. Though what did it matter if he was around or not? It didn't help that she was still confused about why she cared what Mike Burnett thought. So he'd been nice. Mike had always been nice.

She entered the lobby. Ron wasn't there, but a fresh pot of coffee was. And luckily, Maxine was nowhere in sight. Savannah calmly got a Styrofoam cup and poured a quick one then hurried into the elevator before someone stopped her.

Leaning against the elevator wall, she wanted to weep. This trip wasn't turning out to be the serene and healing experience she'd imagined. After wallowing for a few seconds, she realized she hadn't pressed the button. She straightened, hit her floor and took a fortifying sip of caffeine.

She was made of tougher stuff than this. After what Mike had told her, how could she dare think this wasn't the road to closure? And if she encountered a few bumps along the way, she'd just put the blame on Ron. That made her feel a tiny bit better.

Chapter Five

The wind was blowing again and despite the sun shining directly overhead, the cool afternoon air kept things pleasant for Mike and Chip. Not a bad day for moving the rest of the herd to Logan Flats, where they'd have a few more weeks of grazing before winter.

Mike wished he knew when Savannah planned on leaving town. After seeing her at the bakery yesterday, he'd decided it would be best not to run into her again, what with her getting all jittery around him. Though he couldn't help wondering why she'd want to come back to Blackfoot Falls.

It couldn't be nostalgia. And he knew for a fact it had nothing to do with the cabin and land she and her mom had left behind. The bank had owned the property for years. The shabby two-bedroom cabin had never been worth much, but the seventy acres it sat on butted up to Burnett land. At one point he and his dad had considered buying the whole thing. Now, for some reason, Mike was glad they hadn't.

"Dammit." Chip must've jumped five feet. "Why the hell did you let him go? I almost injected myself."

Watching the calf plow past Chip, Mike swore under his breath. The little guy headed straight to his mother. They'd have to catch him again. Cool nights and warm days had produced four sick calves. They all needed antibiotics and to be put in a pen to heal. "Sorry."

"Where's your head at? You've been acting weird all week."

More like two days, but he didn't correct the kid. Mike shaded his eyes and checked to see if Bill and his brother had made it to the mouth of Sunrise Canyon yet. He'd hired the pair to help gather the rest of the cattle that hadn't been relocated yet. Another day and they'd be done rounding up the heifers. He radioed Bill to ask for their head count.

Just over three hundred.

They were almost finished.

"Helluva job, guys. Meet me back at the house by six. I have cash for you." He clicked off. "Thanks for recommending them. They're good workers."

"Yeah, they're pretty quick for a couple of old dudes."

"Shut up," Mike said, laughing. "They're in their forties."

"Yeah, I know." Chip grinned. "What are they…about seven years older than you?"

"And here I was going to ask if you'd like to work here full-time."

Chip's brows shot up. "Are you serious?"

"Not anymore."

"Come on. You know I was just joking."

"I was thinking you could start in about a month?"

"Sounds good to me, but isn't that sucky timing? Will you have enough work for me all winter?"

"Yep. I got a lot to do, so you'll be taking over some of my daily chores." Mike stepped back after they treated the last calf. He'd asked his dad last night about making Chip full-time, and just as Mike knew he would, his dad told him to make the call. "Look, I know you do other odd jobs here and there and if you want to continue, we can work your schedule around them."

"Thanks, Mike." Chip carefully stowed the meds in the metal box. "Actually, I wouldn't mind letting most of those jobs go. Let a high-school kid take 'em. Some of the older folks around here are just plain cheap."

Mike smiled. Most of them were on fixed incomes. He'd never minded doing work for any of the old-timers. They hadn't tried to take advantage. "As for which days you work, I'm flexible. Although I need you to do the morning feeding at least three days a week."

"Hell, I live close. I can do it every morning if you want."

"After a night of pool and beer?"

Frowning, Chip scratched the side of his head. "Okay, I might've jumped the gun…"

Mike laughed. "We'll work it out."

"Hey, you want to go to the Full Moon again?"

Mike knew he should say no. Savannah could have left already. But he had no way of knowing, so there was only one answer.

Chip blotted his sweaty forehead with his sleeve. "Maybe that cute blonde is still around and you'll get lucky."

"What blonde?"

Snorting a laugh, Chip said, "What blonde? The one you were eyeing every chance you got."

"I thought she looked familiar, that's all."

"Right. Uh-huh."

Mike shook his head. "If you'd been paying more attention to the game instead of me, maybe I wouldn't have beaten the pants off you."

That wiped the smirk off Chip's face. "Okay, okay."

"Twice."

"Hey, I almost had you the second time."

"And yet…" Mike's attention was drawn to the silver sedan traveling south on the county road.

Chip turned just as the car passed. "Who's that?"

"I don't know."

"Probably tourists. They're always getting lost looking for old movie sets. Last month I found a carload of them stuck near the creek."

The ill-kept gravel road was almost a quarter of a mile away, but Mike thought Savannah might have been behind the wheel. The sedan looked a lot like the one she'd been trying to avoid yesterday.

He headed for the cottonwood where he'd tethered Dude. "Nobody has any business down here," Mike said, grabbing the reins. "I'm going to go check."

"Want me to go?"

"I've got it. Probably just a tourist, like you said. You might as well head back."

Mike rode straight toward the Rileys' old cabin. Though she could be headed for the creek, he'd start with the cabin first.

Without a clear trail, the area thick with lodgepole pines and overgrown brush, it took him twenty minutes when it should've taken ten, and for all he knew, she was already gone, but once he'd made it to a small clearing, he thought he heard a faint bleat. Slowing Dude to a walk, Mike listened. It was a stray calf, all right. As he dismounted he heard another bleat.

After pushing his way through a thicket of gnarly sage and scaring a grouse, he saw the little fellow, exhausted and wobbling under a small cottonwood. The calf was clearly a late arrival and a runt, probably only a week old. Odd that he'd gotten separated from his mother. He didn't belong to Mike, but it wasn't uncommon for The Rocking J cattle that grazed on public land to stray in with his herd.

Damn, he wished he'd brought the ATV.

Mike doubted the mother was around, since she hadn't responded to the bleating. But he remained perfectly still, trying to listen for her. After a few minutes, he phoned Chip, who hadn't seen any men from The Rocking J. But he agreed to look for their number on Mike's desk and give them a call.

Mike disconnected and inched closer. The calf barely made a sound. And when Mike scooped him up, he didn't struggle.

"I bet you're scared, aren't you, buddy? Let's see what we can do about that." Dude wouldn't be happy about giving the calf a ride, but too bad. It wasn't going to be easy for Mike either.

All legs, weak and panting, the calf allowed himself to be laid on his belly over the saddle. Dude shifted nervously and his ears went back, but Mike soothed him until the gelding finally settled. Mounting was tricky, but he managed to plant himself in the saddle and then wrap the calf's legs around his middle so he could hold on to the little guy.

A low bellow sounded from the direction of the creek, a popular spot for stragglers. He headed toward it. That bellow was from a bull, and not one of his, but the calf's mother might be somewhere close to the bull.

Luckily, the creek wasn't far, but he kept Dude at a slow pace, making sure the little one didn't get jostled too much. The calf hadn't moved much since his first two kicks, which wasn't a good sign. Probably dehydrated. And Mike still hadn't heard the high-pitched call of a momma who couldn't find her calf.

As it turned out, the silver sedan was parked on the side of the trail that led to the creek, but Mike couldn't spare it any attention. His focus was on the calf, and he'd given Dude his head knowing he'd follow the scent of the water.

Then something occurred to Mike. "Hey, no swimming today," he said, leaning down to stroke the gelding's neck. "You got that?" The horse ignored him and picked up speed. "I mean it, Dude."

Mike heard a laugh and looked up, not at all surprised to see Savannah. This had been a favorite spot of hers.

She rose from the rock she'd been sitting on. "Does he ever answer you?"

"No, but sometimes I get the feeling he'd like to." He reined the gelding to a halt.

Savannah saw his passenger and gasped. "That's a... What is that?"

"A calf. Would you do me a favor?"

"Sure," she said, dusting off the seat of her jeans as she warily approached. "Maybe I should've said 'that depends.'"

Mike passed her the reins. "Hold on to these while I get down," he said, lifting the calf in his arms.

"Wouldn't it be simpler to let me hold him?"

"It would if he weren't sixty pounds."

"That's not so much. I'm pretty strong."

"Sixty pounds is a lot of weight, especially—"

She rolled her eyes and reached up for the calf.

Mike held firm and continued, "Especially if he starts kicking again."

"The poor thing looks too exhausted."

"He's also scared."

She tossed back the reins. "I wouldn't offer if I didn't think I could handle him," she said, and moved closer, her attention focused completely on the scrawny, leggy bundle he reluctantly placed in her arms.

"Watch out."

"I see," she said, laughing, her face lit with pure joy as his skinny legs went everywhere. "Oh, he's so sweet."

Dude snorted.

"You are, too," she said with a fleeting glance at him.

Even after Mike dismounted, she held the calf close and stared into his tired brown eyes. He quit squirming and let his head rest against her chest.

Savannah sighed.

"I'll take him now." Mike secured Dude's reins and could tell the big baby wasn't thrilled about it.

"Just point me in the right direction," Savannah said, clearly not about to give up her ward.

"Let's get him closer to the creek, then you can put him down. I want him to call out for his mom. If she's anywhere in the area, she'll let him know."

"Come on, baby, let's get you some water."

Mike shook his head. "He'll only drink from a teat or a bottle at this age. I mean, we can try, but I doubt he'll know what to do."

"Oh," she said, walking carefully, seemingly without difficulty.

Several moments later, Mike put his hand on her shoulder. "This is far enough for now."

"Why?"

"There's a bull around here somewhere. I need to make sure we're not near enough for him to get wind of us. They can be dangerous."

"Okay. I'll watch this guy." She crouched and carefully put the calf on his feet. His little bleat wouldn't travel far.

"I'll be right back." Mike headed out at a jog and heard another bellow, which sounded as if it was coming from farther up the creek.

He followed the water's edge for a bit then stopped and listened. No upset momma. As for the bull, Mike guessed he was up past the second bend. It seemed safe enough to bring the calf so he could try that bleat again.

When he got back to where Savannah was petting the calf, she stood up with a look of excitement in her eyes.

"Did you hear something?" he asked.

"No, but I had an idea. I've got a first-aid kit in the back of the rental car. Sometimes they include gloves. Maybe we could fill one with water and cut off the tip."

Mike doubted it, but, hell, at this point it wouldn't hurt to try. "Good idea," he said. "Why don't you go get it while I check if anyone's seen his momma."

"Sure thing." Her cheeks were pink, her eyes shining. This woman in no way reminded him of that shy, gawky teenager who'd always walked with her head down, her shoulders slumped. She wasn't just pretty, she looked happy and alive.

Chip called to tell him The Rocking J had sent out a couple men to find the momma, and Mike asked him to bring his ATV to the creek. Dude would be happy he didn't have to give the calf a lift again.

Savannah was back two minutes later. "Here," she said, holding the sealed bag of powder-free medical-grade gloves. "How should we do this?"

"First, let's get him closer to the water. Maybe the scent will stimulate his saliva."

Before he could bend down, she'd already crouched and had the calf securely in her arms. Mike noticed her wedge sandals. "I don't want you to lose your footing."

She stood, not wavering a bit. "I'll be careful."

"Okay, but I'm staying right beside you."

She nodded, not even blinking when he cupped her elbow.

It was still a good fifteen feet to the water, most of it over rocky ground. He moved his hand to her back without actually touching her but ready to catch her around the waist if she stumbled.

"Oh, boy." Savannah laughed, even as she struggled to hold on to the now squirming calf. "This little critter must really be thirsty."

"You're making me nervous," Mike said, and relieved her of her charge.

"I would never let him get hurt."

"I was worried about *you*. Look, I've got a knife in my back pocket. Why don't you get it, open the bag then fill the glove with water. I'll get him settled here."

The second he felt her fingers slip inside his pocket, he tensed. Which caused her to pull back. Damn, he hadn't thought this through.

"Should be in there." Thankfully, his voice sounded normal. "It's just a small Leatherman tool."

"Um, okay."

Bracing himself as he felt her hand slide tentatively toward his ass, he mentally started counting backward from a hundred...

The calf raised his head and bleated louder than before. Savannah quickly pulled out the pocketknife.

Mike let out a breath and glanced at her.

A light blush had spread across her cheeks. Turning away, she hurried the last few feet to the creek and filled the glove with water then tied it off.

"Let's use the pointed tweezers," he said, then noticed she'd already found them. "You need a hand?"

"No, I can do it."

He was glad, because the calf wanted to get close to the creek and Mike didn't think that was a good idea. So he held him against his chest, as the poor little guy bawled, until Savannah had pricked the tip of the long finger. Then Mike set him on the ground.

Getting on her knees right next to him, she held the

glove over the calf's mouth, letting the water drip. "Come on, baby, drink up. I know you'll love it once you taste it."

A few seconds later, the calf was slurping loudly on the substitute teat. He wasn't drinking much, mostly just wetting his throat. "You're doing great," he said, more to the calf than her, but she nodded.

"He likes it."

"I can see that. You're now officially his foster mother."

She was staring at him, but when he met her gaze, she looked back at what she was doing. "You're a nice man, Mike Burnett. But you were a nice boy, so I shouldn't be at all surprised."

Mike didn't embarrass easily. But he felt a little warm under his shirt collar. What was a guy supposed to say to something like that?

Savannah solved the problem. "What's his name?"

"I'm not sure he has one," he said, holding back a laugh.

"What? Why not?"

"He's not even mine."

Her blue eyes widened. "He's lost?"

"I think he might belong to The Rocking J, though I can't tell for sure since he hasn't been branded yet. I'm waiting for a call."

"I hate that they get branded," she murmured, so quietly he almost didn't hear her.

No way would he get into that discussion, so he said nothing.

Tilting her head to the side, she lightly stroked the calf's back as she watched him drink. "Where will you take him?"

"Back to my place, unless someone shows up to claim him. Hopefully we'll find his mother soon."

"And if you don't?" She continued to let the water drip, keeping the finger just in the calf's mouth so he wouldn't choke.

"He's going to be fine, Savannah. I promise." He'd almost touched her. Even after catching himself, the impulse was so strong it shook him all the way to the toes of his boots.

It was just that she looked…soft. The smoothness of her pale skin, the honey-blond hair that was pulled into a messy ponytail, even her lips looked soft as they lifted in a gentle smile.

Her gaze still lowered, she angled her head to see the calf's face. "Do you know how lucky you are that Mike was the one who found you? Huh, buddy? I'm going to call you Buddy for now. What do you think?"

What Mike thought was they were sitting too close together for his peace of mind. "Not that you asked my opinion, but I think it sounds just right."

After that, neither of them moved or spoke. He could hear the creek splashing against the rocks, the chirping of a few birds that hadn't flown south yet. And Buddy, of course. The rustling in the brush didn't seem to alarm Savannah. Probably just another grouse.

The ground was littered with red-and-gold fall leaves. A stiff breeze brought down a few more from the sparse branches. It was nice here. Peaceful.

Buddy had turned out to be a great distraction for her. She looked relaxed not tense like she'd seemed the other night.

For that matter, the calf had distracted Mike from all the questions in his head.

Until the sound of an ATV broke the calm.

He got to his feet. "Come on, Buddy. Let's see if anyone's claimed you or if we're going to take a quick ride."

"If you think it would be easier on him, I can take him." Savannah stood up. "We can put him in my car, and I'll follow you to your place."

Trying to keep a straight face, Mike rubbed his jaw. "I don't know about that…"

"It has to be safer and more comfortable." She put a hand on her hip. "So what's the problem?"

"The word's out that I've got the little fellow. You kidnap him and I'm left to face the music."

She narrowed her eyes and then laughingly gave him a light shove.

Pure reflex made his hand shoot out and catch her wrist.

Their gazes met and held for the space of a couple of heartbeats. Then he let her go.

He cleared his throat as the engine noise escalated. "I feel bad enough we interrupted your peace and quiet."

"You didn't interrupt anything. In fact, I was wondering, and maybe you can tell me, when the sun sets this time of year. I can't remember."

He squinted up at the sky. "Not for another couple hours."

"Oh, excellent. I miss watching them. I'm usually busy working. And anyway, there's no better spot than right here," she said, tossing a glance over her shoulder. "It's not even too overgrown."

"Won't your fiancé be wondering where you are?"

"My—" She hesitated and let out a long sigh. "He's not really my fiancé. I wish I could explain more but—"

The ATV turning off the road drowned her out.

"That's Chip," he said, unsure how he felt about leaving this conversation unfinished. He crouched and picked up the calf.

"May I hold him just one more time?"

"He might start kicking," he said, reluctantly, giving her Buddy.

"I can carry him to the ATV."

"Come on, Savannah. Rocky ground, remember?"

She turned a smile on him and glanced at the protective arm he didn't recall raising to catch her if she stumbled. "Yeah, but you've got me, right?"

Mike's chest tightened, and he nodded. "I've got you."

Chapter Six

Savannah dragged the small round table from the corner of her room closer to the bed, where she'd spread out a bunch of photos. Over the past four days, she'd taken more than a hundred pics of the town and the surrounding areas. So had Nina and Ron, and they'd each printed a dozen or so that best illustrated what they'd seen and experienced as *first-time* visitors—without bias—the good, the bad and the ugly.

Those last two subcategories would likely stir up some lively protests and maybe even spark a few tempers. However, people normally settled down when the subject shifted to dollars and cents and how much the merchants could be raking in just by making a few changes.

The presentation was scheduled for tomorrow afternoon and would take between two and three hours. Ron and Nina would give her their comments later, and then they'd fly back to Denver in the morning.

Savannah would rest a lot easier once Ron was gone.

It seemed as though the four days had flown by in a blur. And now she wasn't that anxious to leave. Mike was the reason, of course. No denying that. But not just him. Yesterday at the creek, sitting on her favorite rock, then helping Buddy...it had all been, well, amazing. The serene beauty of the countryside and all the wildness she'd loved as a child hadn't changed. Everything had been just as she'd remembered it.

Mike had been a bonus. She hadn't expected to see him yesterday. A lot of land stretched between his ranch and her family's old cabin. But she hadn't taken into account that the ranchers would be rounding up their herds this time of year. Still, what were the odds she'd have seen him? Well, she knew that answer.

How many times had the image of him riding up with the calf's skinny little legs wrapped around his waist sneaked into her thoughts?

Nope. She wasn't about to go there. Her peace and quiet wouldn't last forever. Ron and Nina had driven to Kalispell to have more photos printed to include with the written report. An end was in sight. Only one more day to soldier through, and then things would be easier.

She'd started sorting the photos when her phone rang. It was Rachel McAllister Gunderson from the Sundance dude ranch. Savannah had left a message requesting a quick peek at the operation for "a future getaway." Rachel was pleasant and accommodating, and not only offered to have Savannah and Ron over later in the afternoon but also invited them to stay for the barbecue they were having for their guests.

Smart. Very smart.

The mayor had mentioned that Rachel was among the very few who were savvy when it came to attracting tourists. It would be good to see what that meant, exactly.

After texting Ron about going to the Sundance ranch, Savannah separated the photos of all the shops on the west side of Main Street. The second she picked up the next stack, her cell phone rang. It was Ron.

"I just texted you."

"I know," he said. "Look, we haven't gotten to Kalispell yet, so we might be cutting it close."

She glanced at the bedside clock. "What's taking you so long?"

"Sightseeing. Anyway, the service stinks out here, so I better make this fast. I want you to meet me at the town square as soon as I get back."

"Why?"

"You're cutting out."

"Why?" she repeated.

"Don't worry, it's work-related."

"Fine." She heard static and disconnected.

Okay, back to work. She glanced at her notes then laid out the photo of The Boarding House Inn, with its white siding, dark green shutters and an inviting porch complete with rocking chairs. The inn dated back to the early 1900s, and the newest owner had kept the flavor of the old place, which had been an actual boardinghouse. The structure had been reinforced, and the cosmetic changes had resulted in a very cute boutique inn that she hadn't expected to find here—though Nina said the rooms were tiny.

Next, she laid down pics of the Cut and Curl and the pawnshop. Another storefront between the two was vacant, just like several others in town. On the upside, according to the mayor, four shops that had closed during the recession had reopened recently.

Her cell phone rang again.

With a sigh, she picked it up and saw it was Mike. She'd given him her number never dreaming he'd actually call. Automatically, she straightened and smoothed back her hair.

Oh, for the love of—"Hello?"

"Savannah?"

"Mike?"

"Got a minute? You asked me to update you on Buddy."

"Yes, of course. How is he?"

"Happy. Back with his mom. But I think he misses you."

Savannah laughed. "Did he tell you that?"

"Not in so many words."

Hearing the smile in his voice made her grin. Nice that Buddy had a home but… "I'm assuming he belongs to The Rocking J, then."

Mike hesitated. "You don't sound too pleased. They're a good outfit. We all lose strays now and again."

"It's not that," she said. "I just…well, I was hoping he turned out to be yours so I'd get to visit him before I left."

Silence, then Mike asked, "When is that?"

"Could be late tomorrow afternoon." Holding her breath, she added, "But more likely I'll fly out Sunday evening."

"Okay, if you're serious, I think I can swing a visitation."

Savannah laughed. "Yes, I'm serious. I am his foster mom, after all."

"He's going to surprise you. They grow fast. By the weekend, you'll have trouble picking him up."

"Wow. That quick?" She probably should leave things alone. What she wanted had little to do with Buddy, cute as he was. Being with Mike had been nice. But what good would come of seeing him again? She lived in Denver, and she'd been hoping this thing with Porter would turn into something. So far they'd only met for drinks or dinner when he'd come to Denver, but there was potential. "I didn't even ask if you had the time to take me."

"I do."

"The thing is, I'm not all that flexible. I have the presentation to give tomorrow…" She trailed off, sighing, when she realized what she'd said.

"Presentation? In Blackfoot Falls?"

Oh, hell, it didn't matter at this point. "Yeah, I'm actually here working. Your mayor hired my company—please, you can't repeat what I'm about to tell you. Okay?"

"Hey, if it makes you uncomfortable, don't tell me anything."

Savannah smiled, not the least surprised he'd offered her an out. "By tomorrow afternoon everyone will know, so I don't mind giving you a preview." Being able to set the record straight about Ron was highly motivating, though Mike deserved the explanation regardless. "Ever heard of a secret shopper?"

"I believe so."

"Well, the company I work for specializes in community branding and tourism marketing. Ron, my so-called fiancé, and Nina, who you met at the bar, and I, we've been secret-shopping the town and even the B & Bs, dude ranches and campgrounds in the outlying areas. Basically, we evaluate the town's appeal and how it could do better to attract tourists."

"Please tell me you'll recommend taking down the tacky Halloween decorations that just went up and continue to surface every lousy year."

Savannah laughed at his dry tone. "Yes, but I'll try to be a bit more diplomatic."

"Huh. Interesting."

"You sound dubious."

"No, it's just…you mentioned a presentation?"

"That's right. I'll summarize our observations, point out where improvement is needed and offer my team's suggestions to the city council and the merchants."

"Do you get many small towns asking for your services?"

"Not this small, no. But the presentation isn't at all confrontational, if that's what you're thinking. Mayor Thompson's goal isn't just to generate more tourism but to keep tourists here long enough to spend some money. So what we do is give everyone, merchants primarily, a glimpse of what we saw as first-time visitors." Realizing how that could be viewed as a contradiction, she added, "It's legit. I was only a kid when I left."

"Yeah, I remember," he said in his easy drawl, then possibly remembering a little too much, he hurriedly asked, "Have you been living in Denver since you left?"

Savannah figured she knew what he was getting at, but he didn't understand the process. "We don't point fingers or shame anyone. We're here to help and we make that very clear from the start. Small businesses generally don't have a lot of disposable income, and keeping that in mind, we try to come up with low-cost solutions. Our presentations are always very well received."

"Well, you'd be surprised at how riled some of these folks get over the littlest thing. I hope Mayor Thompson warned you. I'd hate to see you step into a minefield."

"She explained that some older residents argue for the sake of arguing, but I'm not worried." It was sweet of Mike to care, though.

"I think I'm following. What has me stumped is why pretend you're engaged?"

"Sometimes there's good reason for the ruse if a community is trying to attract honeymooners or destination weddings. This isn't one of those times. Ron's just being a jerk."

Mike laughed. "Yeah, well, I can't say I blame the guy for trying."

Savannah sank to the edge of the bed, glad he couldn't see her blush. Several photos slid to the floor. The way his voice had dipped low and sexy made her pulse flutter. "Um, can we back up to that conflict of interest thing? I honestly feel I've been completely unbiased. But I still don't want anyone knowing who I am, including my coworkers."

"No one will hear it from me."

"Thank you."

"What happens after the presentation? You all pack up and leave?"

"My colleagues are actually flying back tomorrow morning," she said. "We don't all need to be here."

"If you're free after you finish tomorrow, how about having dinner with me?"

Savannah lay back and stared at the ceiling. Would that be inviting trouble? Probably. It was far too easy to picture his dark, penetrating eyes and that slow, killer smile of his. Oh, for goodness sake, he'd asked her to dinner not to have sex.

"I understand," he said after waiting too long for her response.

"Oh. No. I mean, yes. To dinner. That would be great." Her heart had started pounding and she was afraid he could hear it in her voice. Dinner. That was it. If she kept things light and friendly, what was the harm?

"Good. I look forward to it."

"Me, too." Her pulse hadn't slowed one bit. "Guess I should get back to work."

"I'll be rooting for you," he said.

Long after they'd disconnected, she remained on her back, ignoring the photos she was no doubt creasing. It didn't matter. They were only for her file. Duplicates had been set aside for the written report. The digital copies would be included in her PowerPoint spiel. The announcement hadn't been posted outside the city office yet, but the mayor expected a large turnout. A lot of the townsfolk would come out of curiosity, which wasn't necessarily a bad thing. It would be easier all around if everyone was on the same page.

For example, the hideous Halloween decorations.

Savannah shuddered.

It took no time at all for her thoughts to drift back to

Mike. Over the years, she'd forgotten about him. He'd gotten lost in the horrific avalanche of memories of that last week before she'd left. For a while she'd convinced herself the whole disaster had been her fault. If only she hadn't badgered her mom into letting her go to Blackfoot Falls High. If only she'd continued to be homeschooled, her mom would never have met her teachers.

The first affair had begun two weeks after Savannah entered her freshman year. At least Mr. Miller had been separated from his wife. The next two affairs had occurred in rapid succession; and both teachers were married men.

Savannah briefly closed her eyes. A vivid image of the way the other students had stared at her that last day took her breath away. Her mother had picked her up before lunch, but it had been too late. She'd felt like the scum of the earth.

Before she could get swept back into that quagmire, she took several deep breaths. Soon enough, her heartbeat slowed to an easy pace again.

Forcing herself to rally, she picked up the fallen photos. A few minutes later, her phone rang. Again.

It was Porter's ringtone.

"Hey you," she answered. "Aren't you in Paris?"

"Looking out at the Champs-élysées and L'Arc de Triomphe even as we speak. I wish you were here with me."

"I know. Me, too." They both knew that wasn't possible for now. She'd made it very clear she wouldn't go anywhere with him until his divorce was final. He'd felt it was unreasonable and thought having filed the paperwork should count for something. And it had. She never would've gone to dinner with him in the first place if his divorce hadn't already been in the works.

Porter didn't know about her mother, the home wrecker, but he was well aware of Savannah's strong feelings about not becoming involved with a *still-married* man, which was why they'd only had a few meals together, nothing more.

"You could've come with me," he said. "I'd have bought your ticket and had Caroline make dinner reservations for us at Le Cinq."

"If you saw where I'm staying, you'd understand just how much that hurts," Savannah said with a laugh.

"After you wrap things up tomorrow, you could still meet me here."

"Come on, Porter, you know better."

"In fact, let Ron or Nina handle the presentation. Leave now. I'll have Caroline book your flight." Evidently, Porter didn't care for argumentative women.

Too bad. She didn't like it when he ignored her wishes.

"First of all, Ron and Nina are going home tomorrow morning. And more importantly, we're not having this conversation—"

"Clothes won't be a concern. Shopping here will spoil you forever. Whatever you want…consider it a bonus," he said, coaxing her in a very unsubtle way.

Savannah wasn't crazy about shopping to begin with and then to have a man pick up her tab? Oh, that just rubbed her so wrong. "Wait." A comment he'd made finally registered. "How did you know Ron was here?"

"I talked to him the other day. He probably mentioned it."

"Did he call to complain?"

"No." Porter paused. "Why? Is something wrong?"

"Everything is fine. This just isn't our usual type of client and Ron's been—" Savannah stopped herself. When she'd started seeing Porter, she'd vowed to never discuss another employee with him. Or anything that went on in the Denver office unless it negatively impacted the company. Although the casual way Porter had mentioned that phone call made her wonder how frequently he and Ron spoke. "Everything is just fine."

"Good. So about you coming to Paris…"

"Any news on how the divorce is proceeding?"

"If I had anything to tell you, don't you think I would have led with that?" He was never brusque with her. Nor had he been this insistent.

Was dangling Paris supposed to make her change her mind? Did he think she was that shallow? Savannah was becoming too annoyed to care about what he thought. While she couldn't deny being excited that a man of Porter's stature had shown an interest in her, she wasn't stupid or blind to his sometimes overbearing sense of entitlement. His father had been the brains behind the company, which he'd started over forty years ago.

To be fair, Porter was no slouch in the intellect department—he'd earned his Ivy League degree. But having grown up without an understanding of the word *no* had done him no favors.

"Are you there?" he asked softly.

"I'm here, but I should go. I have a lot to do." If he thought she'd cower and not bring up the divorce anymore, he was in for a rude surprise.

"Honey, you're upset with me. I understand completely and I apologize for being curt. It's only because I miss you."

She sighed. "It's been a hectic week."

"So, don't you think some time—"

"Please don't bring up Paris again."

The faint sounds of piano music and voices drifted over his silence. "Forgive me," he said finally. "I understand and respect how you feel about this…precarious situation."

Did he? She wasn't sure, but she was willing to give him the benefit of the doubt, mainly because she felt guilty. It wasn't like her to find fault with every little thing he said.

They'd only started getting to know each other two months ago, and mostly via phone. When he wasn't traveling, which was a lot of the time, he worked in the corporate office in Dallas, and Savannah worked in the regional Denver office. And while their last dinner together had ended in suggestive banter, sex hadn't entered into the picture. He knew she was adamant about waiting until he had that final piece of paper.

Savannah just wished she was still feeling the little thrill that hearing his voice used to bring. Maybe she shouldn't linger here, but that dinner with Mike was too tempting to let pass. He was so straightforward and had a calmness about him that she was very drawn to. A sense of security that he didn't need to prove with money or innuendo. It would be a pleasant change.

Startled at the thought, she almost forgot Porter was still on the line. "I'm sorry, did you say you…"

He left her hanging for several awkward seconds. "I'm at a reception and being summoned to the bar. We'll talk later."

"Yes. Have fun." She wasn't shocked that he disconnected before she finished speaking.

All right. Perhaps she needed to think about a few things pertaining to Porter when she went back to Denver. The unbidden *pleasant change* thought still bothered her.

So did the phone call between him and Ron. It wasn't just Porter's casual reference to it. She had the feeling they knew each other personally. It would certainly account for Ron still having a job. It didn't matter to her, but if Porter had told Ron about them without clueing her in, that would upset her. A lot.

Chapter Seven

After hanging up with Savannah, Mike wondered if she intended to keep her identity secret once the presentation was over. In fact, he wondered why she'd come back here at all? To relive a bunch of bad memories? And worry someone might recognize her? On top of that, he'd bet her boss wouldn't be happy to know that she could've compromised the job she was sent to do.

None of it made sense, but clearly she had her reasons.

Mike roped a calf that had been breathing too hard on its way to join the others in the sick pen, and gave him a shot of antibiotics. He and Chip had finished moving the few stragglers, and then Mike had identified three more calves that didn't seem to be holding up too well. Hopefully this was the last one. He didn't look too bad, but when it came to the fall babies, Mike tended to err on the side of caution.

Once he saw the calf wobble over toward the others, his thoughts drifted back to Savannah. If she felt she had something to prove, he supposed her coming back would make some kind of sense. Except that meant she had to admit who she was. The second she did that, people wouldn't be marveling over her success. Fourteen years would vanish in a heartbeat, as if the scandal that had turned the town on its ear had happened only yesterday. All the trash talk would start up again, about her mom and the Riley name.

Savannah had always intrigued him, that little lonely girl in the old cabin. It was isolated, deep in the woods, without even a marked driveway. He'd never had a reason to go anywhere near the place, except for that time when his dog hadn't come home. Mike had looked everywhere for the crazy mutt. Even though he hadn't gotten all that close to the cabin, he'd heard her parents yelling at each other. It was such a small place, too. Nowhere for a kid to hide or block out the ugly language.

The Rileys had lived out there for as long as he could remember, but he hadn't known her first name. At one point his mom had told him and his sister they should be extra nice to her. But by then Lauren was going off to college and Mike, having just turned sixteen, was right in the middle of his love affair with baseball.

So they mostly hadn't spoken. One time he'd asked her if she needed a ride because she'd been carrying all those books. She'd looked at him as if he were a mystery then scurried off with a shake of her head, her sun-streaked brown hair flying wildly behind her.

After that, he hadn't bothered her. He probably shouldn't have bothered her at the Full Moon either. But he wasn't sorry. Not now that he understood more about what she'd been hiding.

Whatever picture of the town and its people she'd painted in her mind as a child had put Savannah at a disadvantage. And not just for her personally. He couldn't help worrying about how the town would react to her presentation. He didn't care how much she and her coworkers sugarcoated their suggestions, most of the folks around here would interpret it as criticism. They'd shoot down anything these *city people* had to say, even if it made a world of sense.

The mayor had to know that. Sadie Thompson was born and raised here and had to deal with the cadre of old-timers who hated that the clock ran forward. So maybe she and Savannah knew something he didn't, and everything would turn out just fine. As for the few newcomers who'd opened shops recently, they'd appreciate any help to get the town rolling again.

Mike knew the prevailing attitudes weren't unique to the residents of Blackfoot Falls. It wasn't even just a small-town issue. He imagined every community had its share of narrow-minded hotheads who often couldn't agree among themselves. One belief did seem to unite these folks: they all feared that outsiders meant change. And generally, they weren't wrong.

"Hey," Chip called as he rode up on a mild-tempered bay mare Mike's mom had named Penelope. "I finished filling the feed banks in the second pen. If you don't need me, I'm gonna go stack hay."

"Sure." Mike nodded at the pair of sick calves that had worried them yesterday. "They're looking better."

"I thought so, too." Chip wheeled the horse around. "What about tonight?"

"I'll have to let you know later."

"No problem."

Mike watched him ride off, thinking how Savannah would probably like Penelope. Although he didn't know if she'd ever ridden a horse. Her parents might've raised a few chickens but not horses. If Mike remembered correctly, her dad had hired himself out as a hand for the Circle K and then the Sundance for a short time before he laid tracks out of town. He had no idea what her mom had done to make a living when she wasn't homeschooling Savannah.

Damn, he couldn't shake the feeling that Savannah was here to prove something. She might not realize it, but more than likely she'd end up disappointed. Just like his ex-wife.

He and Ellen had married too young, and it had taken

him too long to figure out that everything she did stemmed from wanting to prove something to her parents, to her neighbors. To just about anyone who crossed her path.

She'd thought being married to a professional baseball player would fix everything she didn't like about herself. When the dream had fallen apart, she'd moved on to an ER doctor in Billings. Mike heard they'd divorced last year.

Oh, hell, he had no business thinking about Ellen or Savannah. His mom was right. He'd like to find a nice woman who wanted to be a rancher's wife, and he also wanted kids. He'd like all that to happen while he was still young enough to keep up with them.

Mike sighed. It just didn't seem as though he'd find the right woman in Blackfoot Falls.

Savannah glared at Ron.

He smiled back and had the audacity to slip an arm around her shoulders.

She had a good mind to leave him standing in the middle of the square to deal with Louise from the sewing shop and the Lemon sisters. They were twins, not a day under eighty-five, and they looked adorable in their matching Halloween sweaters—right up until they opened their mouths. The two didn't seem to know how to speak to each other without arguing…at an ear-shattering decibel.

Oh, it was so very, very tempting to simply walk away. Tomorrow everyone would know why they were here, anyway. And she'd bet these women weren't going to appreciate Ron wasting their time like this. What a mess.

"You know," Louise drawled, "if you two lovebirds aren't dead set on a church wedding, I bet we could get Pastor Ray to perform the ceremony right here. What do you think of that?"

"I like it," Ron said, turning to Savannah, his lips pressed thin. "What about you, honey?"

Before she felt confident she could answer civilly, a middle-aged woman with a short, no-nonsense haircut rushed toward them.

"I'm terribly sorry I'm late," she said, her hand extended. "I'm Betsy. My husband and I own the steak house."

Shaking the woman's hand, Savannah didn't bother to hide her confusion. "I'm afraid I'm at a disadvantage here," she said, pinning her gaze on Ron. "You haven't told me a thing about any of this." Let him take the blame when the charade was over tomorrow.

"As much as I'd like to take the credit, this wasn't my idea." He smiled at Louise.

"Oh, it's nothing," She waved him off, flushed and beaming. "I ran into your beau at the diner this morning and found out you two were trying to decide where to tie the knot. So I started mulling it over and thought why not right here. The square looks so pretty this time of year."

She swept a hand to encompass the postage stamp–sized patch of semi-dormant grass, a stone bench, a huge elm tree—mostly bare except for the unsightly ghosts, witches and goblins hanging from its limbs— and a black lamp-post wrapped with cobwebs. The trio of clay pots brimming with yellow mums were nice, but otherwise…it was awful.

"The reception could follow immediately after, without anyone having to drive anywhere." Louise looked very pleased.

"Excuse me, dear—" The twin on the right—Mabel, if memory served—was frowning as she addressed Savannah "—would we have to take down our decorations?"

"We've spent a long time getting them all up," her twin added, her expression pinched. "And we aren't even finished yet." Suddenly the sisters were allies.

"In case the weather was to turn, I suppose putting up a tent wouldn't be out of the question," Louise murmured as her gaze darted over the area.

"I spoke with Kylie, who owns The Cake Whisperer. She sends her apologies for not being here. She's all by herself this afternoon, but she assured me she can provide the cake," Betsy said. "Now, about the hors d'oeuvres—"

"You came late," Louise grumbled. "You can just wait your turn."

A crowd had gathered, and now people were asking questions, throwing out opinions, the men jokingly urging Ron to run and hide before it was too late. Savannah felt as if she'd been dropped into the middle of a sitcom.

What got to her the most? A few women had kindly offered to help, their sincerity touching her someplace deep in her heart. She was starting to dread tomorrow, when they discovered this was all just a sham.

"Everyone," she said, raising her voice above the din and scanning the wizened faces and the few twentysomethings. "You've all been truly wonderful. Unfortunately, the trouble with surprises is—" she made herself look at Ron, going for fondness and hoping no one noticed the daggers "—I made an appointment for us to go to the Sundance and—"

The grumbling started. Like a train that had jumped the track, there was no stopping it. Some folks had misunderstood and thought that the Sundance was in the running as a wedding location. They seemed convinced the town had just lost that particular race.

After thanking Louise and the other women, and without a word to Ron, Savannah walked toward her car. She'd parked in front of the bank, half a block down, and on the way she dug a couple aspirin out of her purse.

Naturally, Ron caught up with her. "Do we really have an appointment?"

"What the hell was that?" she muttered, so angry she couldn't see straight.

"Just doing my job."

"First, we decided this isn't that kind of destination. And second, even if it were, you don't think the timing was incredibly stupid?" She didn't wait for his response. They reached the car and she quickly climbed in behind the wheel before anyone could intercept her.

Apparently, Ron wasn't anxious to join her. The passenger door was unlocked, but he hadn't even opened it. She uncapped the bottle of water she kept in the cup holder and swallowed the aspirin.

For the first time, she wondered if he was deliberately trying to sabotage this assignment. Had he switched places with Duncan to make her look bad? She'd rebuffed his advances, been promoted twice…maybe he had it in for her.

Tapping her fingers on the steering wheel, she considered driving off and leaving him. Despite all his talk about wanting to stay in the field, maybe he felt overlooked. He'd been with the company three years longer than Savannah. Still, she was feeling more and more certain he had a personal relationship with Porter—one that would give him a leg up if he wanted.

Perhaps it was simply that he hadn't played second fiddle in a while and resented it. Ron was used to being the team leader. But then, he didn't have to trade with Duncan.

The more she thought about it, the more the sabotage angle made sense. In four days, they hadn't done anything to make people feel duped. It was something they tried to stay clear of. And then today, of all days, with the presentation tomorrow…

Had he seen her with Mike? Doubtful. And so what if he had? She hadn't done anything wrong.

If he didn't get in the car, she was leaving. She started

the engine, and seconds later he opened the door. She saw that he'd been texting. The stupid jerk had let her wait while he texted someone?

The twenty-minute drive to the Sundance dude ranch was a testament to her willpower. For the life of her, she couldn't figure out why she didn't shove him out the door and leave him for roadkill.

With the blazing orange sun sinking low, the clouds hovering over the Rockies had turned the most extraordinary shades of pink and salmon. Savannah had always loved watching the sun rise from her special spot behind their cabin. And in the early evenings, as she'd listened to the birds and crickets from her favorite rock beside the creek, she'd done most of her reading while waiting for the sun to set.

Denver had many lovely features, and it offered anonymity, which was a plus, but it wasn't the same. She could do without the fast pace.

She'd never thought she would miss anything here in rural Montana.

"Am I going to get the silent treatment for the rest of the evening?" Ron asked.

According to her GPS, she was supposed to make a right turn soon. "You should be so lucky. I'd really like you to explain why you thought it was a good idea to become a public spectacle."

"I already told you. Louise cornered me in the diner. She was the one who got all hyped up about an outdoor wedding."

"She cornered you? And you, who believe you're God's gift to womankind, couldn't have dissuaded her?"

Ron snorted. "If I were you, I'd be more concerned about explaining why you accepted this client in the first place."

"They're paying us $25K. That's not enough for you?"

"Hey, great, and just think, if you'd assigned only two people like you should have, we would've seen more profit."

Savannah caught a glimpse of the Sundance before glaring at him. "Do we have an internal affairs department I'm not aware of?"

"Look out for that rabbit."

She swerved and managed to avoid it. The road had become nothing more than gravel and a few potholes, forcing her to keep her gaze straight ahead. "Thanks," she murmured. Damn him. He wasn't wrong. "So what are you going to do, go running to your friend Porter? Tell him I shouldn't have been promoted?"

At Ron's silence, she couldn't resist glancing at him.

He looked tense but then shrugged. "I've worked for the company a long time. We're casual friends. So what?"

"None of my business. I just don't understand what your problem is with me."

"I have no beef with you, Savannah." He sighed. "I really don't."

The ring of sincerity in his voice unnerved her. She didn't know if she should press the issue or pretend they hadn't just sniped at each other.

They turned down the driveway and as a sizable barn and several other large buildings came into view, the answer was clear. They were on the clock and needed to behave civilly. The Sundance and the McAllister family were both big deals in Blackfoot Falls. Savannah knew that the way Rachel ran the dude ranch was the benchmark for the whole community.

"I don't know if you looked at their website," Savannah said, "but it's pretty impressive."

Ron nodded. "I agree. Nice house coming up on the left. Lots of windows facing the Rockies."

"We're invited to stay for the barbecue. I didn't commit, though."

"Okay, let's play it by ear."

They exchanged conciliatory smiles. A truce. Though only temporary, she was sure.

The aspirin had helped her headache but had done nothing for the sick feeling in her stomach.

Chapter Eight

Ten minutes into the presentation, Savannah deeply regretted not paying more attention to what Mike had tried to tell her.

Ten minutes.

And she was ready to scream.

It didn't matter that the presentation was geared toward shop owners and the city council. In compliance with the town's bylaws, the mayor had no choice but to publicly post the meeting time. Now Savannah understood why Sadie had apologized for doing so. This was crazy.

The room was small to begin with, but the inadequate space hadn't prevented people from cramming themselves into every nook and cranny. It was hot and sticky. They didn't know where to stow their jackets. Tempers were short. A number of the older residents in attendance had hearing problems. Half of what Savannah said, she was asked to repeat.

One city council member was out of town. The other four sat in the front along with the mayor. In the row behind them were the merchants who owned stores on Main Street, as well as the B & B owners. Representing the Sundance ranch were Rachel Gunderson and her sister-in-law Jamie, and they couldn't be a more welcome addition.

Lucky for Nina, she'd left earlier for the Kalispell airport. Much to Savannah's annoyance, Ron had decided to hang around. He was sitting to her right at the card table that had been provided for her laptop and water. At the rate things were going, she'd need a sleeping bag, too. The presentation was going to take all night.

"The importance of curb appeal can't be emphasized enough," Savannah continued, her PowerPoint, running behind her on the ancient screen, showed signs that were ragged or had letters missing and a few buildings with no signage at all. "We have statistics that—"

"I can't hear you." A tobacco-roughened voice came from somewhere in the back. "You need to speak up, girl."

Before Savannah could respond, Rachel got to her feet and turned to the crowd. "Was that you, Earl?" Not a peep. "All right, everyone who wears a hearing aid, raise your hand."

A few people complied.

"Is that it? Really?" Rachel clearly didn't care who got out of line, she called them on it. Everyone knew she was pregnant and short on patience. They didn't want to get her too riled.

Several more hands went up.

"Okay, now, who's supposed to be wearing one but forgot it at home?"

Most of the older folks glanced around at each other, waiting for someone else to go first.

"Come on, people, give me a show of hands if you forgot your hearing aid."

One brave soul did as she asked.

"Well, Ernie, how do you expect to hear what's being said? Evidently you don't, that's fine." She swept her gaze around the room. "As for the rest of you, since you all are wearing your hearing aids, you don't need to be interrupting and asking Ms. James to repeat every blessed thing, do you?"

Lots of muttering, but no one challenged her. Rachel sat and gave Savannah a nod.

Savannah remembered a little about her from the short time they'd gone to the same school. Even though Rachel had been one of the popular kids, unlike the other girls she'd always been friendly. Just as she had when she'd welcomed them to the Sundance ranch yesterday.

"As I was saying, curb appeal," Savannah said, returning to the PowerPoint slide. "Those of you who own businesses here in town might find it interesting that roughly 70 percent of first-time sales come from curb appeal. Now, how that applies to Blackfoot Falls is something—"

A hand shot up somewhere in the middle of the crowd, despite Sadie having asked everyone to save their questions for the end.

But that wasn't what distracted Savannah. Mike had just slipped into the room and found a place along the wall.

Sadie and two council members turned their heads to see what had sidetracked Savannah. She quickly refocused on the arm, now waving frantically.

"Yes?" she said.

A little old man got to his feet. "My wife wants to know—ouch." Presumably the white-haired woman, who'd just smacked his arm, was the wife. "Does all this mean you and your beau won't be getting hitched in the town square?"

Savannah sent Ron a scathing glance, not caring that he looked repentant. She was about to ask him if he'd like to explain it to the audience when Sadie stood and faced the man.

"For pity's sake, Horace. And you, too, Ethel." Sadie nodded at the woman. "You have no reason to be here, let alone ask silly questions." The mayor's gaze swept the room. "From now on, only shopkeepers or those representing them are allowed to ask questions. After the presentation is over. And that's final."

A chorus of protests arose from the audience.

"You all heard me. I don't need to repeat myself."

"That ain't fair," said a man in overalls. "We all pay our taxes, same as the store owners."

The mayor's brows shot up in amusement. "You're sure about that?" She glanced around at all the people who'd suddenly found something fascinating about their boots. "Let me explain one more time to all you stubborn mules. These folks are here to help us attract more tourists. Which means more money for the town."

"That don't help us none," someone grumbled.

"Of course it does, Walt. Don't be such a knucklehead. We wouldn't be sitting in here packed like a bunch of smelly sardines if we had money for a new city hall." A few folks looked as if they took offense to that description, but Sadie didn't stop. "It's high time we made improvements around here. Fix up some of these ramshackle buildings and entice folks to reopen their doors or encourage newcomers to start new businesses. Maybe then our young people will stop moving away in droves."

That seemed to settle down the naysayers.

"But if they're here to help us, why did they have to lie about who they were?"

Sadie let out a sigh of disgust that filled what little space was left in the room.

Savannah didn't see who'd asked the question. Not that it mattered. It had been brought up before, and it was kind of worth it just to see Ron squirm. Yesterday's infantile stunt had brought the curious, as well as the romantic, to the forefront. Otherwise most people wouldn't have noticed them.

But she was more than happy to let the mayor handle

it. She really liked Sadie. Savannah had seen quickly that Sadie wasn't just a colorful character—the formidable fifty-something brunette was the perfect person for the job. She truly was one of them, cared about the town and knew just how to handle the residents.

Savannah looked at Mike, and he gave her a sympathetic smile. She didn't dare smile back. Who knew what people would make of that?

While waiting for Sadie to restore order, she breathed in deeply and thought about the odd connection she felt to Mike. By the time she'd attended the high school, he'd already started college a few hours away. Occasionally, she'd seen him on weekends, and he'd waved from a distance. There was no reason she should feel as if she knew him. Because she didn't. Not really.

Yet he'd never judged her, which said something about him. And he'd admitted to wondering about her over the years. Mike obviously was a caring person. But again, one tiny drop in the bucket of how much she knew about him.

Anyone would think she'd be more astute when it came to relationships. Her parents had married after knowing each other for a week. No two people could be more different. Talk about a cautionary tale. They were married to other people now, and both of them seemed happy. Still lousy parents, but they'd tried.

"I'm sorry about the interruptions," Sadie said, after giving the crowd a time-out to settle. "I should've known better and scheduled the meeting earlier when folks were still doing their chores."

"Please, don't worry about it. We're fine." Savannah glanced at Ron, who was frowning at his watch. He'd changed his flight, and now he'd probably miss it. Served him right for insisting on staying. But it wouldn't serve Savannah at all. "Mayor Thompson, would you excuse me for just a moment?"

Sadie had no sooner nodded when someone else grabbed her attention.

She moved closer to Ron and leaned down. "We're going to miss our flight," he said before she got in a word.

Savannah hadn't mentioned that she'd already changed hers to Sunday afternoon. "Go on ahead. There's no point in both of us being delayed."

"I can't just leave you here."

"I'm a big girl, Ron. I think I can manage without you."

"That's not what I meant. It's just… I know this is partly my fault."

"Yes, it is." She shook her head. "Look, you don't have to give up your weekend. I don't have any plans so if I have to stay overnight, it won't be the end of the world."

Ron sighed. "We only have one car."

"Take it. I'm sure the mayor will get me to the Kalispell airport."

"Hey, I'm sorry," he said, glancing at his watch again. "I really am."

Oddly, she believed him. "Promise me you'll feel like crap all the way to Denver. It'll make me feel better."

Ron laughed. "You got it."

"That doesn't mean you're off the hook. You'll still owe me."

His smile faded. He looked as if he was about to say something, but changed his mind.

"Go," she said. "Be safe." When she straightened, it seemed everyone was staring at the two of them.

She returned to the podium and waited while Ron shook Sadie's hand and said a few words to her. Then he left the room.

"Where's he going?" someone asked.

"He's returning to Denver. I'll be finishing up here with—"

"Denver? Hell, you didn't even kiss him goodbye," the man said. "It's no wonder he ain't waiting for you."

The woman sitting next to him nodded.

Sadie muttered something unintelligible.

Savannah held back a whimper. "Ron is my colleague. He is not—" What was the point? Clearly, these people had selective hearing. "Let's talk about signage. First, I'm well aware that some of the areas I'm using as examples are under the county's jurisdiction. However, it affects all of you. There aren't nearly enough signs telling people where to go or what type of service—"

Smatterings of laughter stopped her.

Not everyone. Just a few here and there seemed to have found something funny about what she'd said.

She paused, waited, her patience slipping.

"We don't mean no disrespect, miss. But we're a small town. We all know where we're going and how to get there. Don't need signs to tell us."

Dumbfounded, Savannah stared at the grizzled older man wearing stained coveralls. He looked dead serious. So did the bearded gentleman sitting next to him.

Sadie stood up and turned a glare on them. "She means signs for visitors, you damn fool."

The men seemed genuinely confused.

Savannah made the mistake of glancing at Mike. His mouth was clamped tight, and he quickly fixed his gaze on his boots.

She was having trouble holding back her own laughter. Afraid she might lose the battle, she looked helplessly at Sadie, who seemed to be having difficulty herself.

"Let's take a short break," Sadie managed to get out to the crowd, then glanced at Savannah. "Ten minutes?"

She nodded and prayed she could hold it together for another minute. Turning her back to the grumblings at Sadie's announcement, she picked up the glass and sipped some water.

"I should've filled that with vodka," Sadie said, wiping a tear from her cheek and eyeing the exodus.

Savannah turned to find half the chairs empty. "Are they leaving?"

"Some are just stretching their legs or grabbing a smoke. Maybe they won't all come back, but I wouldn't count on it. Most of the folks who show up to these things only come out of nosiness."

"I heard that, Mayor Thompson," Mike said as he joined them. "Better not be talking about me."

"Don't you 'Mayor Thompson' me."

He grinned. "I don't understand why you hate that so much."

"Not with everybody. I make Earl and Ernie call me that, or just Mayor." With a little smile, she tilted her head at Savannah. "I asked her to call me Sadie, but she doesn't and I give her a pass."

Savannah had just begun to sober. Why that should set her off, she couldn't say. "Oh, this is terrible," she murmured, briefly closing her eyes to picture Bambi sadly calling out for his mother. That helped.

Rachel walked up to them and bumped Sadie's shoulder with hers. "I have to pee so badly. Do not start without me."

"Go on, girl. We'll wait."

"Hey, Mike, long time no see," Rachel said, walking backward.

"Yep," he said. "Better watch out—"

She backed into a big, broad cowboy and let out a squeal before plowing her way to the door.

Shaking her head, Sadie turned to Savannah and Mike. "Have you two met?"

"Yes." Savannah nodded. "At the Full Moon the other night."

Mike smiled. "You do know Sadie owns the Watering Hole, right?"

"Oh. Yes. Of course. But I've been there, too." She liked seeing him this close, in this light.

They kept looking at each other as if Sadie weren't standing with them. Savannah hadn't noticed before that his eyes were flecked with gold.

She finally forced herself to look away and discovered that someone had pulled Sadie aside. Savannah's gaze returned to Mike's. Had he looked away at all?

"Tough crowd, huh?"

"Oh, my God. These people are—" She abruptly shut up. After a sobering pause as she glanced around, she asked, "Why are you here?"

"Moral support."

"For me?"

"Yes, for you," he said with a crooked grin.

"Thank you." She felt a nervous laugh coming on and breathed in deeply. "I think you missed Rachel dressing down the crowd. Wow, she doesn't pull any punches."

"No, she doesn't. Neither does Sadie."

"I could really use those two. Like, all the time."

"Ah, I think you hold your own." His voice had lowered and they were back to staring into each other's eyes. Like they were the only two people in the room. "Are we still on for dinner?"

Savannah's pulse skittered. "I wish we could leave right now."

A slight frown drew his brows together as he studied

her. "I can't tell if I should be flattered, or if you're that anxious to be done with this town."

"Both," she said, and reminded herself to take a breath. "But mostly you should be flattered."

Chapter Nine

Mike watched and listened to Savannah speak about how the town could increase business revenues and visitor spending. She didn't just point out the problems—and there were plenty—she also offered simple, low-cost solutions.

The woman was impressive; smart, knowledgeable, poised and patient. She remained calm and on point through countless interruptions, many of them silly and inappropriate. It was kind of embarrassing. From the seat he'd found in the last row, he could see some of the town's newcomers exchanging glances and trying not to laugh. Probably wondering why they'd ever moved here while, ironically, Savannah explained the potential for attracting more businesses.

In a way, it was too bad people didn't know who she was. All the longtime residents would remember that nasty piece of business with her mama. Even for a town like Blackfoot Falls that greased its wheels on gossip, the scandal had been a doozy.

None of what had happened had been Savannah's fault, but that must've been impossible for a kid her age to accept. As far as he could tell, neither parent had been a shining example. And then to come out the other end this bright, articulate, confident woman? What were the odds?

The crowd had thinned by the end of the break, and a few more folks had drifted out. Mike noticed people were beginning to check their watches, and he glanced at his. It was getting close to supper time for most. The presentation would've been over by now if not for all the nonsense.

Sadie must've sensed the restlessness and she got up to speak quietly to Savannah. A minute later, Sadie addressed the audience.

"Okay, folks, that's it for today. Ms. James has covered only half the material. You all know why," Sadie said, shaking her head. "But she has graciously agreed to stay the weekend and finish up at a later time."

"Now, you just hold on," Jasper Parsons said, getting to his feet a couple rows in front of Mike. "I've got another question."

Sadie glared at the man, a known troublemaker who opposed boosting tourism, even though it meant nothing to him one way or the other. "Too bad."

"I got a right to ask—"

"Yes, and you'll be free to do so when we reconvene." Sadie turned her back on him. "I'll post the date and time on the bulletin board."

Savannah followed her lead and began packing her briefcase.

"Reconvene," Jasper muttered, half under his breath but loud enough for Mike to hear. "Using fancy words now just cuz she's mayor."

The old guy was bound to cause trouble. He always did. Mike wasn't sure if he should get involved. A lot of curious looks had come his way after folks had noticed him talking to Savannah during the break. Best thing he could do for her was keep a distance for now.

So Mike stayed put. They hadn't settled on dinner yet. He figured they'd go to Kalispell just to get her away from here.

His thoughts went back to Sadie's announcement that

Savannah was staying the weekend. Now that she had unfinished business, it could mean she wouldn't leave until Monday.

Not that it should matter to him. If Savannah had returned thinking she might move back, which was as ludicrous as anything he could've come up with, he would've been first man in line. But she'd never do that, and anyway, he needed a ranch wife, not a career woman, someone who understood the demands of running a ranch.

"Hey, Mike," Sadie called. "Do me a favor and lock that back door. Jasper was just leaving."

Savannah glanced at him and smiled before continuing to pack up, her hair falling forward and hiding her face.

Jasper cursed.

Mike was shocked at how quickly the room had emptied. "Come on, Parsons," he said, pushing to his feet. "You heard the mayor."

"That woman don't deserve the title. Never seen a more piss-poor mayor in all my born days."

Sighing, Mike gestured for the older man to head out.

Fortunately, he didn't argue. He actually seemed more mellow than usual. Might've had something to do with the beer Mike smelled on his breath.

"Now," Sadie said to Savannah, "I'm guessing you two have dinner plans, or I'd invite you to eat with me."

"We do," Savannah said, glancing at him as he walked up. "But if you want to join us I'm sure Mike—"

"No. Thanks anyway." Sadie had always had a streak of mischief running through her, and he wasn't about to guess what she meant by the smile she was giving him. "I'm sure you've taken into account that you won't get a moment's peace eating around here."

"I sure have... Mayor Thompson."

Sadie laughed. "You used to be such a nice boy, what happened to you?"

"He still is." Savannah's quick leap to his defense startled him. And Sadie. In fact, it seemed to surprise Savannah, too. She fumbled the file in her hand and cleared her throat. "Don't chase him off. Mike might be the only person standing between me and a noose in this Wild West town of yours."

"Oh, he's tough." Sadie winked privately at him. "It would take a hell of a lot more than me mouthing off to get rid of him. He'll stick close."

Mike shook his head. "Ever heard the saying 'quit while you're ahead'?"

"Must've missed that one." Grinning, she turned to Savannah. "We'll talk later and figure out how we're going to finish this up. If at any time you decide you want to leave, I completely understand. Anyway, I have the report you've given me."

"Honestly, it's okay. I work in the Denver office not in the field, so I don't have anywhere else to be next week."

"Huh." Sadie drew back to look at her. "Well, then, I guess we're special."

Even before Sadie's teasing remark, Savannah clearly regretted her words. She gave them a quick smile then finished gathering her things.

The three of them walked out together. Mike was glad to see Main Street fairly deserted, which wasn't unusual this time of day. The women agreed to talk tomorrow then Sadie headed toward her office.

"Okay, so, dinner," Savannah said, her gaze sweeping the sidewalk.

"I have an idea about that."

"Good, because I don't. I'm not even sure I have any brain cells left."

"For what it's worth, you did a hell of a job."

She smiled like she didn't really believe him. "I've already extended my stay at the motel. I don't have a car anymore, though, and I need to go dump this stuff." She held up her briefcase and nodded at the laptop case Mike was holding.

"I'll take you to the motel and wait for you. Unless you need some time by yourself."

"No, I'm fine. Not very hungry, though. However, I wouldn't turn down something sweet."

Damn, he was tempted to take that another way. But he knew what that hopeful look was for, and chuckling, he patted his pockets. "Sorry, fresh out. Not even a mint to my name."

"That's okay," she said, sighing. "I like you anyway."

That made him grin…until he noticed Jasper standing outside the Watering Hole talking to Avery. The two of them together always spelled trouble. "I have to ask—do you care if people see you with me?"

"Of course not." She gave him a great smile. "Why would I?"

"I don't know." Shrugging, he steered them toward his truck. "You saw how they are."

"Yeah." Savannah sighed. "To think I used to worry about what they thought of me," she said, then came to an abrupt stop. "Oh, my God. My therapist would be so proud."

Mike laughed. Probably not the best response but he couldn't help it.

"I know. Right?"

"You should be proud of yourself, Savannah," he said. "I barely know you and I sure am." Lucky he held the laptop in one hand and had his keys in the other. The sudden need to touch her caught him off guard. He wanted to feel the softness of her skin, brush the bangs away from her eyes as she blinked up at him. "Not that you'd care."

"Oh, but I do, Mike," she whispered. "I really do."

Mike knew it would be a very long time, if ever, before he forgot that achingly sweet expression on her face as she stared up at him.

"When do I find out the surprise?" Savannah subtly sniffed.

Something sweet sat in the box on the back seat. Mike had volunteered to pick up dinner while she'd stowed her things in her room and changed into jeans and a long-sleeved T-shirt.

"Be patient. After seeing that presentation, I know you've got it in you."

"*Had* it in me. I'm drained. I've used up all my patience for a month."

"I don't doubt it," he said. "You still have to wait."

"That is so mean. Hey—" she glanced around at the familiar landscape, brilliant fall reds, oranges and yellows everywhere, and rows of pines so tall and magnificent you'd swear the tops reached the gates of Heaven "—where are we?"

"Not too far from town."

"I know that much." She thought for a moment. They'd been driving south the last time she'd paid any attention. "We're ascending, aren't we?"

Mike nodded, his smile mysterious.

"Can you believe I've never been on this side of Black-foot Falls? The foothills are beautiful. I can see why Hollywood thinks this place is the best thing since sliced bread."

Mike chuckled. "I haven't heard that one in a long time."

"You can take the girl out of the country, but you can't take the country out of the girl. When did you last hear that one?"

"Not for a mighty long spell."

Savannah laughed. "I surrender. I'd never be able to keep up with you."

Mike lifted his right brow at her. "You saying I'm a hick?"

Studying his strong square jaw, she considered telling him what she really thought. Wouldn't that shock the boots off him? She couldn't help laughing.

"Well, hell." He glanced over at her before turning off the highway onto an unpaved road. "You sure know how to undermine a man's confidence."

"Careful what you wish for…" She echoed the same mysterious smile he'd given her. Although, it might be fun to see how many shades of red he'd turn if she told him he was positively yummy.

"All right. I see what you're doing."

They went over a sizable bump, and she clutched the dashboard. "Okay, now I'm worried the town hired you to do away with me. Jeez. No one will find my body till spring."

"I'm impressed. Good at business *and* creative."

"Aren't you even going to deny it?"

Mike laughed. "I could just leave you out here for the bears. Less hassle and worry for me." Slowing down, he leaned forward and peered over the steering wheel. "Hey, that could come under plausible deniability. What do you think?"

"I think you're crazy. And I blame myself for not seeing that earlier." The whole truck shifted when the left front tire dipped into a hole. "Ouch."

"What happened?" Mike shot her a concerned look.

"Nothing. I'm fine. Just a reflex."

"Hang on. We're almost there."

"Wait." She touched his arm. No, more like gripped it.

Hard. She loosened her hold, let her hand fall away. "There really aren't bears up here are there?"

He looked at her as though he couldn't tell if she was joking.

"I meant…you know, not this low."

Mike frowned slightly, shook his head. "Higher up."

"Right. Go on," she said, gesturing.

The sun had dropped behind the mountains, and the trees around them were creating shadows. Maybe he hadn't frowned at all. Maybe he hadn't seen the blood drain from her face. It was stupid to let her father's cruel taunt play in her head. She wasn't a child anymore.

God, she needed to get hold of herself.

Neither of them spoke for the next few minutes. The silence suited her fine. She wished she could recall the mantras from her self-help CDs. A couple drifted in and out of her brain. They might've stuck if she wasn't swimming in embarrassment.

Mike parked the truck and turned to her. "I should've asked before I brought you up here. I'm sorry."

"What? No." She waved off his concern and looked away. "Don't be silly. This is—" She gasped at the brilliance in front of her.

The vanishing sun had set the sky on fire. Clouds of red and orange streaked across the blazing horizon. Several stubborn gray, pink-tinged clouds hovered over the snowcapped peaks that stretched to the south. The valley between the two mountains formed a V, giving them a window to the incredible display. It was the most glorious sunset Savannah had ever seen.

The company could have had something to do with it… or maybe it was just that he'd been so considerate. Remembering she wanted to see a sunset, listening to her when she said something crazy like "drive" with no questions asked. Accepting her excuses without explanation. He'd even brought something sweet for her because she'd joked about needing it. Despite Porter's lavish spending on meals, he always found a way to insinuate what he wanted in every conversation. And sex was always on the top of his list. Of course he'd pretended he was teasing, and she'd let him get away with it.

But she wasn't going to think about him. Not tonight.

She realized she was holding her breath and let it out with a heartfelt sigh.

"If we'd gotten here thirty minutes earlier, I would've stopped at the first ridge and we would've had a damn near panoramic view."

"Are you kidding? This is perfect." She couldn't drag her gaze away. Finally, she found her manners and looked at him. Mike was staring at her and not the sunset. "Thank you," she said, meeting his darkened eyes. "I can't believe you remembered."

He smiled. "Course I did," he said, lifting a hand and drawing the pad of his thumb across her cheekbone. His touch was so gentle her lids started to drift closed. "You got a smudge here. Probably from all that laughing earlier."

She opened her eyes. "Great." Now she'd embarrassed herself again. "I finished the presentation looking like a clown."

He lowered his hand. "It was tiny."

Her embarrassment ebbed when she realized she would've seen a smudge when she'd checked her makeup after changing her clothes. Mike had looked for an excuse to touch her. The thought made her a little giddy.

She turned back to the sunset. Some of the colors had already faded, and the number of gray clouds seemed to have doubled in just those few minutes. It didn't matter. The sky was still more beautiful than anything she'd seen in a very long time. Perhaps even since she'd left Montana. Her job left little time for sunsets.

They lapsed into a comfortable silence. Just watched nature finish her show, a rather spectacular performance Savannah wouldn't soon forget. Had she ever felt this stress free? This peaceful? Completely in the moment?

Especially after that hellish presentation. She would've been up half the night, pacing her room, wondering how she went wrong.

Savannah was terrible at meditation. But this…this she could get used to.

The last of the sun's dappled light started giving way to shadows before Mike spoke. "Getting hungry?"

"I could be persuaded."

"Do we eat in the truck or outside on a blanket?"

"It's not too cool out?"

"A little. But no insects."

She was worried about the bigger critters.

"Let's just eat right here," Mike said. "I'm comfortable. You?"

Savannah nodded, noting how immaculate he kept the truck's interior. "Do you ever eat in your truck?"

"Not usually." He reached into the back for the food. "But I don't mind."

"I promise to keep the crumbs to a minimum," she murmured, sneaking a look at him.

The way he was stretching made his shirt cling to the muscles in his shoulders and back. No extra fat on him. His movement was slow and deliberate and made her wonder if he knew she was eyeing him. No, there was something in the box he didn't want to mess up, she decided, watching him carefully set it, along with a white bag she'd missed, on the dashboard. Then he reached back once more and retrieved a bottle of wine and two plastic glasses.

"I hope I didn't bruise your arm," she said, just in case he'd noticed her sudden interest in his anatomy.

"When?"

"You know...earlier."

Mike laughed. "That was nothing. Something tells me you have a bear-phobia, though."

"No, it's stupid childhood stuff."

"Tell me." He reached into the back again, this time for bottles of water.

Savannah sighed. "You'll just laugh."

"Maybe."

That he didn't try to deny it made her smile. She looked away, surprised there was still a halo of sunset left. "When I was five or six and my dad didn't want me hanging around, he used to threaten to take me out to the woods and leave me for the grizzlies and coyotes. You know, silly stuff parents tell kids to keep them in line."

Mike frowned.

"What?"

"I wouldn't say most parents do that," he said, his gentle tone bringing a slight sting to her eyes.

She lowered her gaze. As his words sank in, she had to swallow around the lump in her throat when it hit that her father's cruelty had been just that. And once again Mike was being so kind. He could have said so much more, made her feel ashamed. Instead, he'd used kid gloves.

After a big breath so she could speak again, she looked up. "Hey, you know what? I'm starving."

Chapter Ten

"Spread some napkins on the dashboard, would you?" Mike said, passing her a stack he'd pulled out of the bag.

She did as he asked but kept watch on what he was doing.

Setting the bag aside, he balanced the box on his lap. He opened it and pulled out a turnover that was perfectly crisped and filled with something red, maybe cherries or raspberries. Savannah's mouth started watering.

"I should've thought of paper plates," he said, shaking his head. "Not too bright." He was already bringing out something else from the box. A fritter, dark and glistening, that smelled like apple.

"Oh, my God, I don't care about plates."

He might've grinned at her, she wasn't sure. Savannah had eyes only for what had appeared next—a chocolate cupcake, perfectly preserved with every swirl of frosting intact.

She moaned. "You're trying to kill me, aren't you?"

"The lady wanted sweets. I wasn't sure which ones."

"They're all favorites. I swear, I couldn't be happier—"

He pulled out two small but perfect éclairs topped with thick chocolate ganache.

"Okay, now I'm positively giddy."

Mike laughed. "Kylie—she owns the bakery—she's amazing. I admit, I'm a fool for her doughnuts. And these éclairs? Hell, I almost ate one while I waited for her to box everything up."

"Almost?" Savannah gave him a long look. "Come here," she said, grabbing the front of his shirt and leaning toward him until their faces were inches apart. "I smell chocolate on your breath."

Mike stared at her mouth. Probably thought she was going to kiss him. And damn, she wanted to.

Releasing him, she sat back. "I'll let it go this time," she said, her pounding heart stealing some of the glibness she was going for. "But only because you brought enough to share."

"You think so, huh?" His smile was impressively evil.

"Careful. We're way out here with no witnesses, and I can be a real wildcat."

A faint moan came from the back of his throat. He tried covering it up with a cough. That only confirmed her suspicion about what he was thinking. Telling him that wasn't at all what she meant could backfire.

"We have more," he murmured, grabbing the bag and tearing into it.

Inside was a baguette and a couple imported soft cheeses, plus a deli package. "Ham," he said. "Picnic food, right?"

"Picnic banquet."

"Bet you're surprised I could get all this in Blackfoot Falls."

"I've been to the market," she said.

"It's not exactly Whole Foods."

"I didn't say that. They have very fresh produce."

"That they do."

They were talking about groceries—a topic one step up from the weather. All her fault for messing around.

Maneuvering so she was sitting almost facing Mike,

she decided to act like a grown woman…with manners. "Should we start with the cheese and bread?"

"I won't tell anyone if you want to have a cupcake first."

"Nope. Half the pleasure is the wait."

His brows lowered. "I'm not sure about that…" Leaning in just a touch—enough that she held her breath—he picked up the wine bottle from where he'd left it on the floorboard. "I like the getting part."

It wouldn't have taken much to meet him halfway, but no. The waiting was all she was going to have. It was no use thinking about anything else.

"What's the wine?"

He showed her the bottle, and it was one she liked. He could just as easily have brought soda. It was him making her bubbly.

The dashboard served as their table, and their glasses ended up between their thighs. Great fix, but it made her far too conscious of…things.

"I want to ask you a question," she said, focusing on the cheese he was spreading on a piece of the baguette. "But it's important that you know you don't have to answer if you don't want to. Okay?"

He nodded, his brow slightly furrowed. "I made this for you without thinking," he said, handing her the bread. "You can have it or if you'd rather get your own…"

"Thank you." She smiled as she accepted the offering. "After I left, I mean, after my mom and I left, what happened?"

"What do you mean?"

"I mean, what did people say? And, please, if you answer, be completely honest. I'm prepared for pretty much anything."

He tore off another piece of bread then met her gaze. "I'm not sure I can help. I know you don't have any doubt that there was gossip. A lot of it. I was away at college, but when I came home that weekend I heard about some of what happened. Obviously it was big news."

"Who did you hear it from?"

"My mom, though she isn't much for gossip. Meaning she didn't have much to say."

"Do you mind telling me what she heard?"

"Let's see, three of your teachers were involved over the course of two months. They were all married and—well, hell, I'm just repeating things you already know."

"But I don't. That's the thing," she said, aware she was getting anxious. She stopped to take a deep breath. "I only knew bits and pieces and some of it my mom had lied about. I know my English teacher was separated from his wife at the time, and, yes, I did know the other two teachers were married when the affairs started."

"Before all that, weren't you being homeschooled?"

"Yes, my parents thought I'd learn more, but after my dad left, I convinced my mom to let me go to the high school. So she had to meet with the principal and some of my teachers." Savannah shrugged. "I'd tested well. In fact, I could've skipped freshman year, but I didn't want to. I didn't understand why my mom kept having so many parent-teacher meetings because my grades were excellent. What did I know?

"Then one day she came home crying, saying she'd been verbally attacked at the Cut and Curl. Accused of awful things. Still, I went to school the next morning. Everyone stared. It wasn't until she picked me up before lunch that she confessed that she'd lied to me. That she had slept with—anyway, I don't know what became of those teachers. Or their marriages."

Savannah wished she'd waited until after they'd eaten.

Mike had abandoned his food. She hadn't even taken a bite of what he'd prepared for her.

"That day she picked you up at school," he said. "Was that the same day you left town?"

"No, we went home and packed whatever we could stuff into the trunk of the car. I'm not sure if it was by design, but I remember leaving just before dawn the next day.

"I didn't understand the big rush. Nobody ever bothered us at the cabin. I doubt anyone knew where we lived. But my mom claimed the bank foreclosed on the property. At the time I didn't know enough about that type of thing, but in retrospect I doubt there was a mortgage on the cabin. It was already old when my mom inherited it from my grandparents."

His expression thoughtful, Mike took a sip of his wine. "That I might be able to shed some light on," he said after a moment. "Your folks could have used the property for collateral, and the bank called in the loan. Dirk Jenkins was a math teacher. I'm not a hundred percent sure, but I think it was his wife who blew everything wide open at the Cut and Curl. Her father was the bank manager at the time. She might've gone crying to Daddy."

"Huh." Savannah smiled, wanting him to know she was okay with all this. "See? You're helping to fill in the blanks."

Mike studied her for a moment. "Are you sure you want to rip off the scab? The only real takeaway from this is that none of it was your fault."

"I thought it was at first. I mean, I was a kid, and I kept thinking if only I hadn't begged Mom to let me go to school none of it would've happened."

"Savannah—"

"No," she said, holding up a hand. "I know better now. I really did see a therapist for a while, and she was wonderful. She helped me understand it was never my fault. She's the only reason I have any sanity."

Mike smiled. "I have a hunch you did your part as well."

"Now, why would you think that?" she asked, unable to hold back a grin. "It wouldn't have anything to do with me being stubborn, would it?"

"I was thinking more along the lines of persistent."

Savannah laughed. "Frankly, it's good to finally be able to talk to someone who knows what happened and really understands this place. No secret can survive in Blackfoot Falls." She sobered, her gaze drifting toward the mountain peaks. "I've always felt badly about the fallout. And yes, I completely understand it wasn't my fault. I have no residual guilt."

"Had you made any friends in school by then?"

"No. Some of the kids would say hi in the halls. I was very quiet back then and had no social skills to speak of." She sometimes still felt cheated out of her childhood. "I spent a lot of time in the library, which I adored."

"Mrs. Albrecht was still the guidance counselor, wasn't she?"

"Yes, and she was very nice. She tried drawing me out. We might've made progress if all that stuff hadn't happened." Savannah stared at the hunk of baguette left on a napkin in his lap. "I'm sorry. I didn't even let you finish—"

"Don't worry about that."

"Please don't make me feel guiltier than I already do."

Mike smiled and topped the bread with cheese and ham.

Savannah felt pretty good, considering. Nevertheless, she used the opportunity to do a mindfulness exercise. Focusing on her feet on the truck mat, her back against the crease of the door. Really looking at the sky as the edges of the faint light breached the last outposts of rock.

"What about you?" Mike nodded at the untouched food in her hand.

"What? Oh." So much for being mindful.

She took a bite the same time he did then sipped her wine.

After a bit, she asked, "What happened to the teachers?"

Mike refilled their glasses, even though she hadn't had much. "Jenkins was fired, then he and his wife divorced and he moved. Another one resigned. I can't even remember his name, but I know he and his wife left Blackfoot Falls right after that. Mr. Miller must've been the guy who was separated, because he stayed and continued teaching. In fact, I think he retired only recently."

"Did he reconcile with his wife?"

"That, I can't tell you. I'm surprised I've remembered this much."

Savannah nibbled on her food. She didn't think Mike would hold back to spare her feelings, but he might. Funny how he thought he remembered so much. In her mind, the whole event had been huge and indelible. But being in the eye of the storm accounted for that.

The stares of her classmates and some of the teachers had followed her most of her life. She'd been terrified she'd end up like her mother. When she'd found out that Porter's divorce wasn't final yet, she made it clear they could get to know each other, but that was it.

Mike looked worried, though, and she didn't want him thinking she was completely traumatized.

She reached over and touched his hand. "I'm sorry if I've upset you."

"Upset *me*?" His expression relaxed, as did those broad shoulders. "I'm just frustrated that I can't remember anything more to tell you."

She wasn't quick to pull back, especially when he ran

his thumb across the inside of her wrist, gently, slowly. She doubted he was even conscious of it. In fact, Savannah was counting on it, since her pulse had picked up speed.

She didn't want him to stop. His touch felt soothing, safe. It wasn't as if they were doing anything wrong. "You could finish telling me what your mom said. I promise I'm fine."

His thumb stilled. He frowned. "Savannah, the only thing she told me was that it was a real shame that you had to be dragged through the whole mess. That a sweet kid like you shouldn't have to suffer for your mother's lapse in judgment. That's all. I'm not trying to dodge the question."

Of all the times, after all the perfectly good reasons she'd had to indulge herself, *now* her eyes had to fill with tears?

BLINKING, SAVANNAH JERKED BACK.

"Hey…" Mike tried to catch her hand, but she was too quick. Damn, he'd been too quick himself. He probably shouldn't have reacted. If he'd pretended not to see the way her eyes glistened, she would've pulled herself together.

He hoped he hadn't just ruined the evening.

One thing she must've learned well growing up in that cabin, with those parents, was how to retreat. And now that he'd embarrassed her, she'd likely do just that. But not if he could help it.

Hearing a soft sniffle, he decided to take a calculated risk. "I thought you said you were fine."

She turned a startled look at him. "I am." She blinked and sniffed again then narrowed her eyes. "I know what you're doing."

"Yeah? And what's that?"

"It's called manipulation." She sniffed again. "And here I thought you were such a nice guy."

"You weren't wrong." He shrugged, noticing how her

posture changed again. Back straight, chin tilted up. Ready to put on the boxing gloves. "Generally speaking."

There wasn't much light, but it didn't stop her from studying his face. "How did you know?"

"Know what?"

"Oh, come on… That I'd bounce back after you challenged me."

"I didn't, not for sure. But I was hoping real hard."

With a soft laugh, she dabbed at her right eye. "Thank you."

"Okay, I'm going to go out on a limb again—you're welcome?"

She stared down at her wine as if she'd forgotten about it, then took a sip. "Say any mean thing to me you want, but shower me with kindness and I'm toast. Your mom—" Savannah cleared her throat "—your mom's a kind woman, and she raised a kind son."

Mike quietly cleared his throat and gestured to the dashboard of desserts. "Is it sugar time?"

"See? You do know me." She leaned forward while finishing off the last of her bread and cheese, her gaze sweeping the spread. "I can't decide."

"I want one of those éclairs. As for the rest, feel free to go to town." He smiled when Savannah did. "I'm not playing down what happened. It was a big deal. But I think you'd find most people sympathized with you."

"I don't know about that. Something else I learned in therapy—not all parents are great role models."

"True. Guess I'm lucky. Both my folks are terrific people, and I've always gotten along with my sister. But having good parents doesn't guarantee a bright future for a kid."

Savannah had been reaching for the cupcake, but she stopped and looked at him. "What happened?"

"I'm not speaking from personal experience… It's just life isn't always a smooth road."

"It's okay," she said. "I wasn't trying to pry."

He felt like a jerk. He didn't talk about himself often. Most of his conversations were about cattle or the weather or just listening to Chip go on about his girl. He preferred it that way. But after Savannah had laid herself open to him, it wouldn't kill him to share a small part of his own struggles.

Ah, hell.

"I was married," he said. "Right after college."

"You were?" Savannah sank back. "I was wondering how—oh, sorry, I didn't mean to interrupt."

"No, go on."

She shook her head. "Please."

"Ellen and I hooked up in college in Billings. I'd known her for a while, though. Her family owns a big ranch and the Green River Feedlot in the next county, where we used to weigh our cattle before shipping them. We'd run into each other occasionally growing up, but I hadn't seen her in several years.

"Anyway, college was a busy time for me since I was there on a baseball scholarship."

"Baseball? No kidding." Savannah leaned back. "And a scholarship no less. You must've been good."

Mike shrugged. "Most guys around here are into football or rodeo. For me, nothing beat baseball. I've loved the sport since I was old enough to hold a ball."

"Did you—" Her eyes widened suddenly. "Please don't tell me Ellen made you quit."

Mike smiled. "Nope. She came to every game. Cheered me on. Was sure I'd make it in the bigs. We got married right after graduation, while I was still being considered for a farm team."

He paused for some wine.

Dear Reader,

IT'S A FACT: if you answer 4 quick questions, we'll send you 4 FREE REWARDS!

I'm not kidding you. As a leading publisher of women's fiction, we value your opinions… and your time. That's why we are prepared to **reward** you handsomely for completing our mini-survey. In fact, we have 4 Free Rewards for you, including 2 free books and 2 free gifts.

As you may have guessed, that's why our mini-survey is called **"4 for 4".** Answer 4 questions and get 4 Free Rewards. It's that simple!

Thank you for participating in our survey,

Pam Powers

To get your 4 FREE REWARDS:
Complete the survey below and return the insert today to receive 2 FREE BOOKS and 2 FREE GIFTS guaranteed!

"4 for 4" MINI-SURVEY

1 Is reading one of your favorite hobbies?
☐ YES ☐ NO

2 Do you prefer to read instead of watch TV?
☐ YES ☐ NO

3 Do you read newspapers and magazines?
☐ YES ☐ NO

4 Do you enjoy trying new book series with FREE BOOKS?
☐ YES ☐ NO

YES! I have completed the above Mini-Survey. Please send me my 4 FREE REWARDS (worth over $20 retail). I understand that I am under no obligation to buy anything, as explained on the back of this card.

235/335 HDL GMYE

FIRST NAME	LAST NAME

ADDRESS

APT.#	CITY

STATE/PROV.	ZIP/POSTAL CODE

Offer limited to one per household and not applicable to series that subscriber is currently receiving. **Your Privacy**—The Reader Service is committed to protecting your privacy. Our Privacy Policy is available online at www.ReaderService.com or upon request from the Reader Service. We make a portion of our mailing list available to reputable third parties that offer products we believe may interest you. If you prefer that we not exchange your name with third parties, or if you wish to clarify or modify your communication preferences, please visit us at www.ReaderService.com/consumerschoice or write to us at Reader Service Preference Service, P.O. Box 9062, Buffalo, NY 14240-9062. Include your complete name and address. SE-218-MS17

▲ If offer card is missing write to: Reader Service, P.O. Box 1341, Buffalo, NY 14240-8531 or visit www.ReaderService.com ▲

BUSINESS REPLY MAIL

FIRST-CLASS MAIL   PERMIT NO. 717   BUFFALO, NY

POSTAGE WILL BE PAID BY ADDRESSEE

READER SERVICE
PO BOX 1341
BUFFALO NY 14240-8571

NO POSTAGE
NECESSARY
IF MAILED
IN THE
UNITED STATES

Savannah gulped hers down. "Am I going to need chocolate for this?"

"Don't worry," he said as he refilled her glass. "It's a happy ending, but help yourself."

She grabbed an éclair, never taking her eyes off him. "I don't see how, but go on."

"I'd been juggling a lot, going to classes, studying, practice, going to games and trying to spend time with Ellen. What suffered the most were the times I should've been here helping my dad with the ranch. Baseball season is also the busiest time for a rancher. My dad encouraged me to stick with the game, but I knew he was having trouble keeping up, even with part-time help.

"I had to take a close look at what I needed to do. When I got the offer from the farm team, it was a tough decision. Sure, I would've liked to continue to play baseball, but at what cost?" It shocked Mike when he realized how much he was telling her, but it didn't stop him. "I've always liked ranching, and by then I had ideas about how we could improve the place, increase the herd. Just because a farm team picked me up, it wasn't a sure bet I'd be called up to the majors. So, I decided to come home, where I'd always known I'd end up. But Ellen, she went ballistic."

Staring out at the mountains, he vividly remembered the day he'd sat her down to explain his line of thinking. So long ago, yet it was clear as day. "Before you get the wrong idea, let me say that I tried to discuss it with her," he said, turning back to Savannah. "But she refused to listen. Even when I told her that I wasn't good enough for the majors."

Savannah let out a soft gasp. "But how could you know? You'd gotten a scholarship and everything..."

Mike shook his head. It didn't surprise him that she'd reacted exactly like Ellen had. "I knew. Deep down there wasn't a doubt in my mind. I was a young guy used to physical labor but I was already struggling with my pitching arm. It was damn hard for me to admit I didn't think I could cut it, but Ellen didn't care." He shrugged. "Turned out for the best—pretty quickly she decided she liked my being a baseball player more than she liked me."

"What an idiot."

Mike burst out laughing. "Not really. She'd just expected something I couldn't deliver. And…she'd grown up pretty spoiled, I think. I should have guessed when I saw she drove a fancy sports car to school. Living on a ranch wasn't exactly her thing."

"Well, I guess. That doesn't make her smart, though. You two got divorced?"

"Yup. It was a short, disappointing two years. I'd always imagined my life differently."

"Any regrets?"

"No," he said without hesitation. "I really do love ranching. I pretty much run the place now. My folks are in Florida for the winter, and they're going to move there soon, probably in the next couple of years. They like being with their grandkids, and I'm happy for them."

Savannah took another bite of her éclair. "Well, my parents got married shortly after they met. It was a huge mistake. They're both remarried now, happily, from what I can tell. We don't talk much."

Mike wasn't surprised at that, but it was nice to know second chances could work. If one found the right woman. His gaze lingered on Savannah's pretty face and her intriguing blue eyes.

The way she looked at him was something different. Not like the Sundance guests who were in the market for a cowboy—any cowboy. And not like the women that he'd known most of his life.

Savannah had a fascinating mixture of innocence and

worldliness, not unexpected given her background. But that same worldliness was what took him out of the running, not that he'd ever really had a chance.

She took the last bite of éclair, leaving a bit of custard on her lower lip, and for a moment he watched the tip of her tongue make the custard disappear like magic.

He would have liked to have been the magician.

"Aren't you going to have some?"

His head jerked back, hitting the window with a smack. "What?"

"Dessert." She looked at him a little sideways.

"Right." He grabbed the remaining éclair and downed it in two bites.

Her laughter was sweet and soft...at first. But then it got louder. Trying to control herself, she motioned toward his mouth. He looked in the rearview mirror. Clinging to his upper lip was more than a little custard. Grabbing a napkin, he made sure he got everything before glancing her way. Now it wasn't her laugh that was soft but her gaze. As if he'd done something special.

"Want some more wine? Toast the stars?"

She leaned forward and looked up. "Ah. I miss this, too. I always loved the night sky when I lived here."

"Yeah. Guess there's some advantages to living in the boonies. My folks bought us a cheap telescope when we were kids. I always felt so small when I looked through it. I think it helped my perspective of life, though."

"You seem awfully steady and content."

He coughed. "Don't hold back. I know I'm as boring as dirt."

She leaned in, touching his cheek with the palm of her warm hand. "No, you aren't."

When her eyes widened and she started to move back,

he took hold of her wrist, unwilling to end the moment so quickly. A puff of breath caressed his chin.

"It's all right," he whispered.

"Is it?"

Leaning toward her, his gaze sliding from her eyes to her lips and back again, he said, "God, I hope so."

She didn't stop him. In fact, they met in the middle. Their lips touched. Tentatively, he let things be, wanting her to set the pace.

Her mouth was soft beneath his. Her lips parted and she touched her tongue to his slowly, almost shyly. He felt the warmth of her sigh, and then she was kissing him back.

SECONDS TICKED BY, and she could've sworn she could feel the rotation of the earth. When she'd thought about returning to this slice of her past, she'd never imagined *this. Him.*

He was nothing like the guys she'd dated. Not that she was a femme fatale, but she'd gone out with a variety of men. Almost all of whom wanted things to move at whatever pace they deemed fast enough. Not with Mike, though.

Unfortunately, the thought pulled her out of the moment. Naturally, Mike let her go instantly.

"You okay?"

"Better than," she said, making her smile as warm as she felt. If she could have, she'd have given her brain a good shake. "Hey, it's getting late, and you have to get up early."

"Not *that* early," he said, frowning. "Speaking of the ranch, are we going to go visit Buddy tomorrow?"

"Yes. I'd love to. Although, I'm sans car."

"We have three options. I can drive you to the Kalispell airport now so we can get you a rental."

"Option two?"

"I can take you to Kalispell in the morning for the car."

"And door number three?"

"I pick you up tomorrow morning, and you spend the day with me on the ranch. You wouldn't need a car for that."

"Or I can rent a car and I still spend the day with you. If I won't get in the way of your chores."

He looked shocked. "You're not going to work with me? I've got a great little horse that you'll fall in love with."

She laughed. "No. I'm not. Although I promise to watch avidly as you do whatever it is you do."

"You've got no idea what happens on a working ranch?"

"Whatever I learned, I got from the movies. Sorry."

"You grew up in cattle country."

She shook her head. "I grew up adjacent to cattle country."

"Huh. So, you really want to go back to the motel?"

"No, but I should."

Nodding, Mike corked the wine bottle that was still half full before he started the truck.

"Hey, wait, what's the happy ending?"

Mike's smile flashed white in the moonlight. "I'm sitting here with you, aren't I?"

Chapter Eleven

Savannah made a face. What was that awful taste?

One minute she'd been having the most pleasant day-dream and the next...

Her gaze landed on the tube of sunscreen. "Yuck!"

She was supposed to be applying the lotion not skimming a finger over her lips and replaying last night's kiss.

When her cell phone rang, she dived across the bed to grab it off the nightstand, only to realize it was Sadie.

Savannah hoped the day she and Mike had planned wasn't about to go down the drain, but whatever Sadie wanted had to be top priority. "Good morning."

"You sound chipper," Sadie said with a rusty chuckle. "I half expected you'd be at the airport—well, hell, I should ask first. Are you still in town?"

Savannah laughed. "I'm a little insulted you thought I'd desert you."

"Honey, if you'd hightailed it to Kalispell last night, I wouldn't have blamed you one bit."

"And throw you to the wolves? I would never do that."

Sadie snorted. "Some folks around here think I'm the wolf. I just remind 'em not to vote for me next year. How about meeting me for some coffee? Or breakfast. Have you eaten? The diner should've cleared out some by now."

Savannah glanced at the bedside clock and held back a

sigh. "I've already been to the continental breakfast down in the lobby, but coffee sounds good."

"What time works for you?"

"How about five minutes?"

"You must've rolled out of bed early."

"Sorry. I didn't mean to rush you."

"Nah, I've been sitting in my office since seven thirty."

Savannah hesitated, mentally debating her next question. "Will this be a working meeting?" When Sadie wasn't quick to respond, she worried she'd sounded off-putting. "I don't want you to feel obligated to entertain me."

"Well, officially, no. Being as I haven't invited any city council members, I can't rightfully conduct city business. But I wouldn't be surprised if a few shop owners were to stop by our table."

Savannah grinned. It was no wonder she liked Sadie. "Okay, so when are you thinking would be a good time? I do have plans this afternoon, although I can cancel…"

"No, don't do that. I was going to offer to drive you to Kalispell to pick up a rental, but I'm thinking you have that covered."

"Yes, thanks. And I haven't booked my flight yet. I can stay through Tuesday if need be."

"That won't be necessary. Maybe we can get this wrapped up so you can leave tomorrow. Let's see how today goes. Then I'll check with the council members. I know two of them would rather be off hunting. A written report would be fine with them."

They agreed to meet in thirty minutes, and after they hung up Savannah called Mike. She offered to cancel if the change in plans screwed his day up. Luckily, he wouldn't hear of it, and they agreed he'd come by the diner in two hours. She doubted she'd be able to sit still any longer than that knowing he was waiting in the wings.

She gathered a notebook, some copies of her report, sunscreen, her jacket and her tote bag so she wouldn't have to come back to the motel.

It was a pleasant ten-minute walk to the middle of town. The Food Mart parking lot was crowded, even though Saturdays in a ranching community didn't mean the same thing as it did for city dwellers, since few people worked traditional days and hours. The market wasn't very big, though probably adequate for the size of the town. It was just that her memory had painted a different picture.

Slipping off her sunglasses once she entered the diner, Savannah found Sadie and another woman sitting in the back at the largest booth there. Both of them were dressed casually, like her.

Sadie waved. Savannah nodded and as she got closer, she recognized Sally, the owner of the Cut and Curl. Sadie waved again, but it didn't seem to be at her. When Savannah looked behind her, she saw Mallory, the bartender from the Full Moon, and Kylie from the bakery.

Oh, God. Savannah hoped she didn't get a warm rush every time she thought of a pastry. And Mike.

Assuming they'd be following right behind her, she gave them a quick smile and continued on to the table.

"Well, we sure could've timed this better," Sadie said dryly. "This doesn't look like a planned meeting at all, does it?"

Savannah was just about to slide in next to Sally, but stopped. "Did I get it wrong?"

"No," Sadie said. "My fault. Please. Sit."

"Hey," Mallory said, and sat next to Sadie.

Before Kylie could squeeze in, the waitress, Doris, brought over two chairs. Kylie took one and left the other one against the wall.

"Can I get you ladies some coffee?"

Mallory nodded. "Please."

Kylie scooted the chair closer to the table. "None for me, Doris."

"Says the woman with the fancy espresso machine," the waitress said good-naturedly. "How many of those sinful lattes have you had today?"

"One too many." Kylie patted her tummy. "I'll be paying for that stupid machine long after I make the final installment."

They all laughed, mostly in sympathy.

"What about you, hon? Coffee?"

"Thanks." Savannah smiled then looked at the rest of the group. "Nice to see you all."

Mallory chuckled. "You sure about that?"

"Yes. Although if anyone can't hear me, I'll send you emails to recap."

That got a laugh out of them, and then something caused Sadie's expression to sour. "For crying out loud, what's that old buzzard doing in here this time of day?"

They all turned.

"Who?" Sally asked. "Abe?"

He'd stopped to talk to the waitress manning the counter. It seemed he'd been about to take a seat until he noticed them. Scowling, Abe headed toward their table, his shuffling gait not slowing him down.

Savannah recognized him. He owned the variety store and was also a city council member. "Shall we scrap business talk?"

Sadie shook her head, her gaze fixed on Abe. "We're fine."

"How come I wasn't told about this meeting?" He folded his arms across his narrow chest and glared at Sadie. "My opinions aren't good enough?"

"Be quiet, you old coot. We're not having a meeting. You see anyone here from the council?"

Scowling, he swept a gaze from face to face. "Sure looks like a meeting," he said, lingering on Savannah. Good thing she hadn't brought out her notebook or the report.

"Hey, that's not a bad idea, Abe. If you're not too busy, how about you pull up a chair and join us," the mayor said, glancing at the one against the wall.

His frown eased.

"I know we can't have an official meeting." Sadie lowered her voice. "But since these gals are business owners like yourself what do you say we discuss Ms. James's findings?"

"Shouldn't the other members be included?"

"You know how some of those mules are...they aren't all reasonable like yourself. Wouldn't hurt to hear what Ms. James has to say without being interrupted a hundred times. Sally, you mind taking the chair and letting Abe sit next to me?"

He sure seemed to like that idea. Savannah wondered if he had a thing for Sadie, and if he realized she'd just played him like a fiddle.

A couple of the women reached for their coffee cups. But the mayor turned her attention to Savannah. "If that's all right with you."

"Sure. I'd be happy to."

Abe claimed his seat, a smile brightening his ruddy face.

"Oh, there's Gladys," Sadie said. "She owns the River Bend B & B." Sadie made a show of waving the woman over. "I wonder if she'd like to join us."

Savannah joined Mallory in hiding a smile behind her coffee cup. The mayor had missed her calling. She was quite the actor.

Gladys came straight toward them, her salt-and-pepper

hair pulled back into a tight braid. She frowned when she noticed Abe, but she caught on quickly and managed to squeeze into the booth.

"I have a couple questions for Savannah," Kylie said. "If that's okay with everyone. Celeste is minding the shop and I know it's busy, so I need to get back soon."

"Well, let's get started." Sadie glanced at Abe. "Is that all right?"

"Don't see why not," he muttered, flushing all the way to his receding hairline. "If Ms. James is willing."

"Of course, but please, call me Savannah." Something occurred to her. "Mayor, I have a few copies of my written report. Do you want me to pass them out, or would you prefer to wait?"

"I say pass them out." She again looked at Abe, who nodded.

Savannah was glad to sift through her tote. Sadie was more than a good actor, she was a consummate politician. "There aren't as many pictures in the report, but it does have all the pertinent facts and what we think might make the town a place that will encourage tourists to stay awhile. Who knows," she said as the copies were passed around, "one day Blackfoot Falls might become a real destination location and not just a rest stop."

"It already is for the women who stay at the Sundance," Gladys said, mischief in her dark eyes.

"Well, sure, we got a lot of handsome cowboys living in the area. Maybe we ought to find more of them," Sally said, grinning and smoothing her teased hair. "Rounding up a few more mature cowpokes wouldn't be a bad idea either."

The women all laughed.

Looking disgusted, Abe muttered something about them all being sexist.

"To be honest, I would use that in campaigning for a

certain target group," Savannah said. "Rachel Gunderson did just that by including candid shots of her brothers—her very good-looking brothers—on the Sundance website. You all know how well that worked for her dude ranch."

"Truth be told, it turned out good for most of us," Sadie said. "The girls who stay at the Sundance come into town and spend money. And now, so do most of the hired men who used to run off to Kalispell looking for entertainment."

A woman named Alice, who was considering opening a B & B, joined them ten minutes later.

Two hours had passed by the time Savannah had finished her pitches—tailored to each business's particular needs—including her idea for the co-op for the B & Bs. The questions had been excellent. She heard about Kylie's upcoming expansion and how Sally wanted to turn the Cut and Curl into a real salon with all the trimmings. In fact, Sally wanted to know how to find out if folks other than the Sundance guests would take advantage of the extra services, so they discussed surveys and focus groups.

All in all, the business owners understood what was at stake and how each of them could encourage more traffic. The big problem seemed to be about the internet and their presence on it.

But that discussion was more or less led by Sadie, who reminded everyone what a website had done for the Sundance ranch and agreed to talk to the city council about advertising online and offering tourism promotions.

Savannah hit her caffeine limit after her third cup of coffee. She looked at her watch and realized Mike would be picking her up any minute.

Apparently, Sadie caught her checking the time and said, "Okay, we don't have much longer with our friend here, so any last questions?"

Gladys nodded. "Would you recommend I put up my

own website, or can I just do something on Facebook to collect reviews?"

Savannah tackled the excellent question, knowing Gladys, and most of the people here, didn't have the expertise or extra money to maintain a website. Her recommendation to use a committee approach on Facebook got a lot of attention, but that stopped suddenly when everyone at the table looked behind her.

"Speaking of good-looking cowboys," Sadie said.

Turning, Savannah watched as Mike walked through the diner with that loose stride. In his jeans, blue Western shirt and black Stetson, he made her pulse flutter.

"Should I come back later?" he asked, taking off his hat to greet the crowd.

"Nope," Sadie answered. "We've bothered her enough for today. She's all yours."

"Then I'll take her." Mike's eyes met Savannah's and he smiled.

"Hell, I wish you'd take me," Sally said, and pretended she was insulted when the others laughed.

Savannah was just grateful the attention had been diverted from her—and the alarmingly inappropriate physical reaction she was experiencing. She knew she should say something, perhaps offer to answer any further questions, but she simply didn't trust her voice.

Finally, she picked up her tote and took out her wallet.

Sadie snorted. "Oh, put that away."

"Expense account," Savannah said, and laid down two twenties. "Is this enough?"

"This ain't the city," Abe said.

"Right." Savannah smiled. "Though Doris deserves a good tip, since we monopolized her table. Mayor, we'll talk later about Monday, all right?" Getting a nod from Sadie,

Savannah added, "Now, I must go learn about what real ranchers do. My ignorance seems to be vast."

"Hey, I never said that." Mike put his hand on her lower back as she stepped away from the table. "Trying to make me look bad?"

"Impossible," she said, and belatedly realized she really needed to watch herself around him.

After exchanging goodbyes, they made their way to the door, under the watchful stares of the lunchtime crowd.

"HER NAME'S PENELOPE."

"She's a beauty," Savannah said, petting the horse's neck. Penelope bobbed her head and whinnied softly.

"Feel like getting in the saddle? I promise she's gentle as a kitten. That's why she's my mom's favorite."

Savannah shook her head. "I don't think I'm ready for that yet. I mean, she seems very sweet, but she's also very big."

Mike grinned. "You mean horse-sized."

"Scary-sized."

"It's fine." Mike wouldn't push. Anyway, they'd be having lunch soon. "Would you like to meet some of the other horses before we head back to the house?"

"Is Penelope the only girl?"

He laughed. "No. We have another mare. Her name is Amelia Bedelia."

"Your niece's horse? Or are you a fan of the series?"

"Right the first time. Come on."

On their way toward the back of the stable, Mike stopped in front of Amelia's stall and waited for Savannah's reaction.

Her jaw dropped. "How tall is she?"

"Just under eighteen hands. Penny is a little under fourteen."

"Wow. Who does she belong to?"

"Everyone loves Amelia. They all ride her."

At a knock on the open stable door, they both turned toward Chip.

"Lunch is served. I've got beer and I think there's some soda left," he said, looking at Savannah.

"Beer's fine with me," she said.

Chip, wearing a black apron, saluted Savannah with the hand holding a pair of big tongs before he left.

"Hey, I'm sorry about lunch," Mike said as he steered them outside, keeping some distance from Chip.

"Why?"

"We hadn't talked about it, and I figured we'd eat out somewhere. But the minute Chip heard you were coming, he insisted." Mike had no idea why. She and Chip had barely spoken at the creek.

"It's so nice of him."

Something finally occurred to Mike. "We could be guinea pigs," he said. "Chip likes impressing his girlfriend. This might be a practice run so beware."

Savannah grinned. "I think it's sweet. I'm going to rave about the food no matter what. And after we eat, will you have work to do?"

"Nope. I'm free for the day."

"Oh."

Mike stared at her. She didn't look disappointed, but she sure sounded like it. "I don't know how to take that."

"I was hoping to watch you do some real cowboy stuff."

He laughed. "Like chewin' on some tobaccy and spittin'?"

She shuddered and moved closer, almost touching him. That was encouraging. He put a hand on her back, tempted to lean in to see how she reacted. Just thinking about kissing her amped up his pulse.

"I still want to visit Buddy. I mean, he probably thinks I abandoned him."

"You're right. He does. He told me so this morning."

"Don't laugh," she said. "I have a gift with animals. Cats and dogs love me to pieces."

"Course they do. They're not fools."

SAVANNAH DIDN'T HAVE to exaggerate about Chip's cooking. The ready-made sides may have been courtesy of the market, but the ribs were outstanding. "I swear, Chip," she said, patting her mouth with a napkin, "you are a genius with a smoker. How did you learn to cook like this?"

He preened a bit. "It's got to do with timing and the right kind of wood."

Mike cleared his throat.

Chip rolled his eyes. "It's my dad's recipe. He got it from his dad and so on. He put the ribs on yesterday. I finished them here this morning." He glanced at Mike. "Come on, it's not like all I did was heat 'em up. I had to brush on the sauce and everything."

"I didn't say a word." Mike patted his stomach. "Savannah's right. They're good."

"That's an excellent legacy," she said. "I bet your girlfriend loves that you can cook."

"She's always telling me I should expand my horizons. But that's because the only thing she knows how to cook is enchiladas and breakfast smoothies."

"Not that you mind," Mike said before giving Savannah a smile. "He talks a lot about her, smoothies notwithstanding."

"Yvette works real hard, is all. She's not only going to be a hairdresser, she's learning to do manicures and, after she saves up, to do permanent makeup."

"Good for her. Are you two planning on staying in Blackfoot Falls?"

"We'd like to, especially now that Mike bumped me up to full time. It'll be hard on Yvette, though. She'll have to drive to Kalispell to work in a salon."

"I don't know if Mike told you why I'm here," she said, and Chip nodded. "I've recommended that the town step up their services in order to accommodate tourists. Many of the business owners have been receptive, so I wouldn't be surprised if more work opportunities open up for people like Yvette."

"That'd be great." Chip looked from Savannah to Mike and back again. "Can I tell her?"

"Remember, nothing's written in stone, but sure." Savannah had been careful with her wording. Her suggestions were public knowledge, but she couldn't speak for the merchants, and she certainly didn't want to give anyone false hope.

"I appreciate it, Savannah. She'll be totally excited."

"I don't know about you two," Mike said, "but I'm stuffed. How about you and I go over and check up on Buddy? We can drive, unless you want to brave the horses."

"No, the truck is fine. But I should help Chip—"

"No, ma'am," Chip said. "I'll clean up, and then I'll take care of the water troughs."

"Thanks, Chip," Mike said, nodding. "Lunch was really good."

Savannah walked out of the kitchen a little more slowly than she should have. It was such a nice, homey space. The curtains looked handmade, and were beautifully done. The table was one Mike's dad had built himself and later, in his teens, Mike had built the matching hutch. Every trinket, every decoration, and even the plates, had some kind of story behind them. The family and the home seemed inseparable.

"Hey, you okay?" Mike had stopped ahead of her, just off the porch. "I'm sure Buddy wouldn't mind if we didn't go see him until tomorrow."

"No, I'm fine. Better than that, actually. Thanks for showing me the house. It's so nice."

"It's not going to win any design prizes, but yeah, it's cozy."

"It's a home. A real home. One that must have been wonderful to grow up in." She heard the wistfulness in her voice and hoped Mike hadn't.

"Didn't you say you had a condo in Denver?"

"Yeah," she said, as they continued their walk to the truck. "I like it. Open floor plan, lots of windows. I wouldn't call it a home, though." Where had the sudden lack of enthusiasm come from? She really did like the place she'd searched months for. "It fits my needs for now."

Mike nodded. Thankfully, he didn't voice the question in his eyes.

She didn't want to think about the old cabin, or the apartment that had lost its luster in the span of a few minutes. Whatever was wrong with her, she'd better snap out of it.

Chapter Twelve

About twenty minutes into the drive, the urge to take Savannah's hand still wouldn't leave Mike. He glanced at her again, and she seemed to be thoroughly enjoying the scenery. It was beautiful out here, something he took for granted too often.

Lunch had been easy, and even though he'd been robbed of a couple of hours, he'd done some chores so he had more time to spend with her now. He couldn't wait to see her reaction to Buddy. He'd put on a lot of weight once he'd found his mama.

"Have you really been to the Denver stockyards?"

It took him a second to recall what he'd said at the Full Moon. "Yeah. I've been to a couple of rodeos because of my mom, actually. She's got a brother out there, and he's one of the managers of the stockyards."

"I think they have quite a few annual rodeos around that area, but I've never been."

As they passed the road to her family's cabin, he saw her head turn. "I was gonna ask," he said, "if you'd like to drive by the old place. Take a look at it. I don't think it's in great shape. No one's lived there since you left. But it's still standing."

Her forehead crinkled a little. It might have been a risky

question, but it didn't seem as though she minded. Just that she wasn't sure.

Before she could answer, her cell phone rang. She dug it out of her pocket, and the little crease on her forehead deepened. "It's someone from work. I'll call back later."

"Don't mind me. Go ahead, if you think it's important."

Savannah shook her head. "I doubt it's critical," she said, then put the phone back in her pocket. "It's also my day off, and I'm busy enjoying the drive."

He smiled, looked at her hand on her thigh and resisted once more. He wanted her to set the pace today.

She stared out the side window, leaving a pleasant silence between them. But not five minutes later, her phone rang again. She didn't seem thrilled.

He kept his eyes on the road in front of him.

"It's my boss. Sorry." She answered, "Hi, Porter."

Mike did his best to ignore the few brief comments she made, although he couldn't mistake the tone.

"We discussed this," Savannah said, her voice a little louder. "Besides, I'm not done here. I might not even leave until Tuesday."

There was a pretty long stretch of silence before she said, in a much quieter voice, "We'll have to discuss it another time. I'll let you know as soon as I'm back at the office. All right? Okay, bye." She scowled at the cell before putting it away.

Her mood had definitely shifted.

Mike hoped she didn't want to return to the motel.

"Sorry," she said finally.

"Don't apologize. It's work. I get it." Damn, he hated asking, but... "Look, do you need to go back to town? If you do, I understand."

"No. Absolutely not. I deserve this time off."

"From what you've said, today's meeting was a success."

"That's true." She gave him a smile that reached her eyes. "And I can't think of any other way I'd rather be spending today than with you."

SAVANNAH TURNED AND leaned against her door so she could watch Mike.

"Cows are really good mothers," he said. "His momma was distraught that she'd lost him in the chaos of the herd being moved, and we knew the second she scented him at The Rocking J. She started bawling, and Buddy bleated right back. They didn't quit the conversation until he was in the pen. She licked him so hard, she knocked him sideways twice."

"That's so sweet. I wish I could've seen that."

"Oh, you'll see plenty. We're less than ten minutes away."

She listened to the cattle lowing, but her thoughts returned to earlier in the drive, when she'd considered asking Mike if he was planning another trip to Denver. Of course, that was when Porter decided to call. Why was he trying so hard to get her to Paris? Did he think she'd let down her guard, forget he wasn't divorced yet and sleep with him? He was a persistent man, but she was losing her sense of humor. It was especially tricky trying to talk in front of Mike, who was as courteous and attentive as Porter wasn't.

She'd always known he didn't like being told no, although until now, she'd thought she was the exception. Getting involved with him, no matter how innocently it had begun, was beginning to feel like a mistake. He wasn't just her boss, but the CEO. It wouldn't be pleasant, but as soon as she could manage a face-to-face, she needed to have a talk with him.

Returning her attention to Mike helped her feel relaxed and, oddly, inspired. "Does Twin Creeks do any advertis-

ing? Like for their motels or restaurants? I didn't see anything online, but I wasn't surprised. I know it's smaller
than Blackfoot Falls."

"I haven't been there in a while, but I don't think they
have a motel. I heard someone opened a barbecue joint.
And maybe a pawnshop. They've always had a small gro-
cery store and a hardware store that supplies the nearby
ranches. I doubt they've spent anything on advertising."

She'd only taken a cursory look at the surrounding
towns, because they were so tiny and remote, but now that
she was here, it wouldn't hurt to poke around. "What about
Greenville and Munson?"

He smiled. "Oh, man, they make Twin Creeks look like
a big city. Again, it's been a while. Greenville has a gas
station that also sells soda, snacks, sandwiches, that kind
of thing. There's a counter in the back that serves as a post
office."

"How long since you've been there?"

"A couple of years."

"What about Munson?"

"Same deal. I remember going to Munson on a field trip
in middle school to look at the dinosaur tracks."

"Dinosaurs?"

"Dinosaur, actually. There are only two footprints.
Granted, they're big ones. They said T. rex, but I don't
know."

"See, now, they can make something out of that. Are
the tracks on private property or on government land? Are
there signs?"

"Public land. I think there's a sign pointing in the general
direction, and for a buck you can buy a map. Once you get
a few yards past the tracks, there's a marker that explains
there were dinosaurs all over northern Montana. Though I

happen to know most of the noteworthy excavations have taken place farther east, around the Hell Creek Formation."

"I vaguely remember hearing something about that." Savannah's mind was already working double-time. All of these little extras in the area could help Blackfoot Falls. It was a stretch but she had the time to investigate.

"Like I said, though, it's been a while. But if you want to check Munson out, we can drive over there now. There's also an abandoned gold mine about fifty miles south. Or we can take a longer trip there tomorrow."

She almost told him to head for the highway, but thought twice. "I'm really excited to see Buddy. And I don't want to cut that short. That being said, I don't want to monopolize your day tomorrow either."

Mike smiled. "You think about when you'd like me to pick you up in the morning, and we'll be tourists together."

"What time will you be done with chores?"

"Early. Shortly after daybreak."

"Oh, that is early." She was looking forward to spending more time with him. She wasn't going to say that, though. Not with the echo of Porter still in her head.

"Is something wrong?" he asked.

"Not at all, why?"

"That sigh was pretty big."

She hadn't even noticed. "No, I'm fine. Just thinking."

Which she went back to doing, although on a different subject. She already knew the population of Blackfoot Falls as a whole wasn't terribly enlightened. If anything could be launched in that place, it would all have to come down to individual efforts. Or, if they were really smart, they'd reach out to the other towns and expand the improvements-by-committee ideas across the board. Supporting each other so that all of them could win.

"Not too far now. Have you seen Buddy yet?"

Savannah laughed. In the distance, she could see a large number of cows that, according to Mike, were the first-calf heifers and the more mature cattle, who wouldn't compete for the feed. To her, that just meant lots of babies, but she was sure she'd be able to spot Buddy. She secretly hoped he'd spot her first.

"How do you tell the cattle apart?"

"We don't. We watch out for the breeders, replacement heifers and calves, of course, and make sure the whole herd stays healthy. This is a stressful time, preparing for winter. You probably remember how bad it gets around here, and cows don't like the wind."

"What, you put them all inside when it gets really awful?" Too late she realized it was a stupid question, but Mike didn't laugh or anything.

"No. There are natural windbreaks, and we also have portable shelters. We give them different feed, enough to build up their fat stores, and we lay bedding so they don't get too cold. But these cattle are bred here and they grow thick coats."

"Are the babies going to be outside all winter?"

"We're extra cautious with them. When it's not too bad, they'll learn to get tough."

"This is much more interesting than I'd imagined."

"Yeah, like watching paint dry."

"I'm serious. I'm a bit distracted because of Buddy, but I'd love to hear more." She spotted a calf and grinned. "Will you know him on sight?"

"I might," Mike said, but she heard his hesitation. "He's still scrawny, so he shouldn't be too hard to find."

He slowed down on the rutted road next to a big pen. It was larger than the one she'd seen that morning at his ranch. There were a lot more cowboys working, too. Mike parked the truck on a scraggly patch of grass.

She got out but waited for him to come around, and then he walked her not to the pen but to the corral behind it. There were about fifteen cows there and the same number of calves. She saw two runts, but she knew Buddy immediately. "There he is."

"That's him, all right."

Savannah had gone to her knees to reach in and touch the calf, if only he would look her way and come closer. "Buddy," she said, her voice high, the way she called to dogs at the park. "Here, Buddy. Remember me? I carried you to the creek. When you were lost. If you come here, I'll pet you, you big boy."

She knew Mike was behind her, but when she turned to look at him, he wasn't alone. Two other cowboys around Mike's age were standing with him. All three had their arms folded across their chests, and two of them were trying to hold back their laughter. Mike's pressed lips told her they'd been teasing him before she'd turned around.

If they thought they could embarrass her, they had another think coming. She went back to talking to Buddy.

Behind her, though, she heard Mike say, "Shut it, Larry."

"Hey, I didn't say nothin'."

"Say nothin' quieter. Even better, go back to work."

Her next call to Buddy got him to look at her. He bleated. Loudly. She was thrilled. "Come here, baby. Come, let me pet you, honey. Remember me? I helped you find your mommy. Who is very, very pretty."

Mumbled laughter wafted over her, but she ignored it in favor of watching Buddy take several sturdyish steps toward her. Some of the larger calves were scampering around and taking a few running steps, and she worried they would knock Buddy over. "Come here, sweet pea. Come on."

He came toward to the fence, bawling and bleating the

whole time. Every step, he said something else. Maybe that he remembered her. And when he got closer, Savannah ducked partway under the rail, leaning in far enough she was able to scratch his little head.

It must have surprised him, because he shook like a wet dog, but then he took another small step and let her scratch him again.

That was all, because Mom came to investigate, and she didn't seem pleased to see Savannah. So she wormed backward out from the corral and took Mike's hand as he helped her up.

"He came right to me," she said, keeping her voice low so the other guys wouldn't make fun. "Did you see? He let me pet him."

"I know. I think he did remember you."

She couldn't help her excitement, and before she even thought about it she'd grabbed hold of Mike's shirt and kissed him right on the lips. He kissed her back, slowly at first, and then what had started as a thank-you turned into something a lot more intense.

She felt one hand go to her nape as the other settled on her waist. She let go of his shirt to slide her arms around his neck. When she parted her lips, he slipped his tongue inside her mouth, slowly stroking hers.

The sound of someone clearing their throat in a vulgar way made her pull back.

"Thank you," she whispered, keeping her lips close to Mike's ear. "Thank you so much. Not just for bringing me, but for not making me feel foolish."

"Who, me?" he said as soon as he could look her in the eyes. "I'm a total sucker for newborns and calves. Chip calls me an old softy."

"Not that you're old, but I already guessed you were a softy."

"You did?"

"It's one of the things I liked about you way back and even more now."

"Huh," he said. "I'll remember that. Despite the human company, it was well worth the trip."

"Are they friends of yours?"

"Sort of. They're just jealous. Probably never saw a woman as pretty as you."

"Ah, now you're just sweetening the pot," she said, stepping back. "And trust me, you don't need to."

"Just speaking the truth. You ready to go?"

"Absolutely." They walked next to each other all the way to the truck, bumping shoulders a few times. Neither of them gave the gawkers a second glance. She even let Mike open the door for her and give her a hand up. The tingling lasted until they were on the main road.

Chapter Thirteen

Mike was having trouble keeping his eyes on the road. All he really wanted was to watch Savannah. Not only had she kissed him like she meant it, she looked happy and animated, and she'd been talking the whole way back. Mostly about her presentation on Monday, but he didn't mind.

He noticed her looking expectantly at him, and he remembered she'd asked him about the towns south and west of Blackfoot Falls.

"Everything that you've mentioned to me makes sense," he said as he turned onto the road that led to his place. "I'm sure you're right that the bigger towns on the way to Glacier National Park are cashing in on the tourists. I do know there are a couple of motels along Highway 93, but they're nothing special, and I think both of them are motel-gas station hybrids. The only advertising I've seen, other than for the park itself, is from Whitefish. They've got a number of hotels and, I think, a resort. They're about twenty-five minutes from Kalispell. But I don't do much traveling out that way."

"Visiting Greenville and Munson tomorrow will help me view Blackfoot Falls in context. I can't see how anyone could argue with bringing in more tourists dollars."

"Look, I'd love to tell you no one could mistake your plan for anything other than a great opportunity..."

"Yeah. I know. Yesterday was tough, but this morning's meeting gave me new hope. Seriously, everyone had something to contribute and their questions were savvy. You know, this is the smallest client we've ever taken. But if handled correctly, and if Sadie can get the town behind the effort, it could end up being even more successful than I thought initially. Who knows, smaller towns along the way to big vacation destinations could end up a whole new type of client."

"Well, if anyone can pull it off, I bet it's you."

Savannah laughed.

"I mean it. I don't know many people who would still be so gung ho after dealing with that bunch of idiots yesterday. You could've handed Sadie the report, said good luck and got the hell out of Dodge. I know I would have."

"I doubt that."

"Oh, yeah, without a second thought. I have no patience for that kind of crap."

"Huh. Okay. Yet another side to you." She laid her head back, looking at him and smiling. In the next instant, she straightened. "Do you know if Twin Creeks or the other towns have movie sets, also?"

"I heard the last movie crew built an old ghost town somewhere near Minersville. Sadie might be able to fill you in more. I didn't pay much attention to the movie folks."

"Thanks, I'll ask her. Did you know that 69 percent of all family vacations are road trips and 49 percent of all vacations are to national parks, with 42 percent driving to theme parks?"

"No, I must admit I didn't, but those seem like significant numbers."

"They are. Just thinking about that side road you took me on last night to look at the sunset…can you imagine if it was easier to get there in a sedan? Or if there were signs? I wonder how many views like that can be seen between towns."

Mike decided it was best not to comment. He understood the economic advantages of her plan and how tourism could really help the town, but he liked Blackfoot Falls as it was. Quiet, opinionated, close-knit. Progress was fine with certain limits.

Places like the one he'd taken her to last night should be held sacred.

"You know what? I changed my mind," Savannah said but didn't elaborate.

He glanced over at her. "About?"

She was frowning at something in the distance. "I wouldn't want anyone going to our spot." Turning sharply to him, her eyes widened. "I didn't mean *our* spot. I meant—"

"I agree." He reached over and squeezed her hand.

A blush had spread across her cheeks. "While I'm on a roll, can I change my mind about something else?"

"Go for it."

"I was considering taking you up on that whole riding-a-horse deal." The smile she gave him could've melted butter, though she didn't need to convince him to prolong their day. Twice now, they'd kissed. He'd like to make it a lot more.

"Happy to oblige. But I'm curious…why the change of heart?"

"I'm not sure." She looked at him with a baffled expression.

He pulled up between the barn and stable and parked. "Did you bring a jacket?"

"Yes."

"So all we need to do is get you a hat. I think I have just the one that'll make you feel like a regular cowgirl."

She opened her door. "Oh, lord. What have I gotten myself into?"

Mike held back a grin. He had an idea or two. But he wisely kept them to himself.

THE STABLE SEEMED stuffier than it had earlier, the smell of leather more pungent.

"I don't need cowboy boots?" Savannah asked. She was stalling, although she wasn't going to back down. Not completely. Frankly, a sudden rainstorm wouldn't be amiss.

"The ones you're wearing have the right kind of heel, even if your toes don't squish together until you want to cry."

"Careful. You almost left out an important part of the experience."

"I think your imagination can fill in the blanks. You about ready?"

She pulled the borrowed Stetson down on her head and zipped her jacket up higher. "As I'll ever be."

"Good," he said, steering her toward the already saddled and bridled Penelope.

"First, come up right next to her and take the reins in your left hand. Make sure the right one is a little tighter than the left."

"How come?"

"It helps prevent the horse from swinging away."

She needed two tries, but then she nailed it.

"Make sure the leather is facing you, so it'll lie flat against the horse once you're on board."

"Okay."

"Now grab hold of a tuft of mane with the same hand as the reins."

"Won't that hurt her?"

"Nah, she's a sturdy old girl." He bent over just enough that his cupped hands bridged right under the stirrup.

After a deep breath, Savannah did as instructed then looked at his hands. "Don't they make special step stools for this?"

"Maybe, but that's not usually called for on a working ranch. We climb on horses young."

"I'm too old for this, aren't I?"

"Not even a little. Come on. You can do this. She might settle a bit, but you're so light she probably won't even feel you up there."

"You're such a liar," she said. It was time for her to just do this damn thing. If anything happened, Mike would save her. She put her foot firmly onto his hands, tugged on the reins the way he'd shown her, flung her right leg over and sat.

Penelope shifted under her, which was an odd feeling, but she wasn't as frightened as she'd thought she'd be.

"Hell of a job," he said. "Like a real pro."

He jumped on Dude's back with so little effort she shook her head. "A real pro, my behind."

He laughed. "Ready?"

At her nod, he started walking Dude nice and slow. Penelope followed. The horse's movement was more something to get used to than to be afraid of. It did stretch her thighs, but she was fit enough that it didn't pull.

"You doing okay?" Mike asked, staying a couple feet ahead but keeping a careful watch.

Savannah nodded, clutching the reins tightly and listening to the crunch of gravel beneath the horses' hooves as they headed west.

After a few minutes of silence, Mike slowed until he was at her side. "Am I making you nervous?" he asked.

"No, I want you close."

"You got it."

His voice had dipped low, and she was tempted to look over at him, but she was trying to avoid any unnecessary movements.

"What do you think so far?" he asked.

"It's not terrifying."

"That's it?"

"We haven't gone faster than a meander yet."

"Do you want to?"

"No."

His chuckle warmed her more than the jacket. "Whatever you feel comfortable with. Even if Penelope decides to get a move on, you're still in control. If you don't like something, tug the reins toward your stomach—but not too hard."

She tried the maneuver, and Penny only took one step before halting. "Thanks. That helps."

She gave the horse a nudge, and they came up beside Mike and Dude. It was getting less scary by the second. Mike was so calm, it helped her loosen up.

The sounds on the range were fascinating. Different, not just from the big city but from her memories. The wind whipping the trees she was used to, but the lowing of cows created its own texture and steady rhythm. She hadn't expected it to be so soothing. She was beginning to understand why people liked trail rides.

"I didn't even ask where we're going." Taking a chance, she looked up and saw that the sky was starting to color. A huge swath of blue sat on the horizon, but the sky above it was turning the clouds a fiery red and above the clouds a very dark orange. "Oh, my God."

"Yeah." Mike's voice was just loud enough to carry.

"You knew this was going to happen?"

"The timing worked out just right. I wasn't planning on anything in particular."

"But this is the whole sky," she said. "Like you talked about last night."

"I was hoping you'd see this before you had to go back. I bet you remember this from when you were a kid."

"Were those sunsets this vivid?"

"Not that much dust or pollution between here and the Rockies to dim things."

"It's perfect. I wish I had a camera."

"Don't you have your cell phone?"

She looked at him briefly before returning her gaze to the sky. "Yes, but I want to remember every second of this and honestly, I don't think a picture could do it justice."

He nodded, moving Dude closer to Penelope. "She likes you," he said.

"I suppose she told you that?"

"No, but she's got that easy gait that tells me all I need to know."

"I'm glad. And flattered."

The more they rode, the more colors erupted around them. It was an extraordinary feeling. The panorama wasn't one she'd seen from the cabin or the creek. Too many trees. But this… She'd always known Montana was called Big Sky Country, and now she understood. Even seeing the silhouettes of the trees in the distance, the jagged outlines of the mountains, was like being allowed into a sacred place. The peacefulness inside her was different than anything she'd ever felt before.

She didn't turn her head, but she knew Mike was right there. If she wanted to, she could put out her arm, and he'd be able to clasp her hand. "This is utterly perfect. I'm so glad you convinced me to take a ride."

"I didn't do any convincing. You got up there all on your own. I've known a lot of people who let fear stop them from riding horses their whole lives. It's says a lot about you that you took the reins."

"I don't tend to think of myself as courageous. Determined, yes, but that's different. But maybe I play it safe too often. Now that I know what I could be missing, it would've been a terrible shame."

"It would have," he said, the sudden huskiness in his voice spreading heat to her core and limbs. "Probably shouldn't miss out on the sunrise either."

She didn't have to ask if he meant what she thought he meant. She wasn't ready for that big a step. Not yet. Although she had the feeling it might have been a night she'd never forget.

Chapter Fourteen

Savannah blinked at her laptop screen. She had more work to do, and though none of it was necessarily required, it would be helpful to Sadie and the rest of the town. And, yes, she was looking to wow them.

Besides, she needed something to keep her from thinking about Mike. And about how her Saturday night could've been very different if she'd given him the slightest sign she was interested. Unfortunately, she kind of was. More than kind of. But there was Porter. Maybe she was being too touchy. It wasn't as if they were in a relationship—in fact, she'd decided a relationship wasn't going to happen. So there was no reason to feel badly for thinking about Mike.

She'd been so tempted to spend the night. It was far too easy to imagine waking up in his arms then bundling up and going outside to watch the sunrise with him. But she hadn't, and she kind of regretted it.

No, she'd done the right thing. After all, she was *on the clock*. Although it had occurred to her that she still had vacation time. She could stay on a few more days.

As she went back to her investigation of the towns around Glacier National Park, she saw a picture of a baby moose, which made her remember Buddy and their wonderful visit. Of course she'd acted like a silly kid, and she understood why those guys had laughed at her but honestly,

Mike had been perfect. It helped that he'd seen her in work mode and knew she didn't make a habit of being childish, but his expression had told her that there was still a lot of kid left in him, as well.

Which didn't mean he was immature. There were several men she knew who fit into that unattractive category. Porter's pout came to mind. She'd seen other women react to it, going all goo-goo-eyed and acting a little silly, she knew he'd eaten it up. That would never be her.

A photo of a cabin, completely unlike the one she grew up in, came on-screen. This one was high-end, a ski-in, ski-out hideaway for the very rich and most likely famous. It made her wonder about her family's old cabin. She'd loved it and hated it while she lived there. The best times were when it was cold outside and she was warm in her bed, covered by her mother's handmade quilts, the sounds from outside just loud enough to lull her into fantasies instead of fears.

Yes, sometimes it got terrible, when the windows rattled and it felt as if the roof would cave in. When her parents fought.

Then her father had left. She'd been sad and relieved. It was a mixed bag, living in those isolated woods. She hoped that by the time she went back to Denver, the predominant memories would be good ones. There had been so much beauty and so many amazing discoveries.

The phone rang, and she nearly fell off the chair in her eagerness to grab the cell from her nightstand. It turned out to be Sadie.

"I hope I'm not calling too late."

"It's only eight thirty."

"Well, maybe I should've waited till morning to give you the bad news."

Savannah's heart sank. "What is it?"

"The city council wants more than a written report and asked if you could finish the presentation on Monday."

Savannah relaxed. "No problem at all. Frankly, I planned on it."

"Look, it's got nothing to do with you personally. I know exactly who kicked up a fuss. It's Thelma. She's the council member who missed yesterday's presentation. She gets back tomorrow night. God forbid anything should happen around here without her dipping her fingers into the pot."

"I promise you I don't mind." By Monday, she'd have her research and her whole pitch put together. She knew it wouldn't impress everyone, but she didn't need it to. It would knock the socks off of the business owners—and of the city council, if they had any real interest in their town.

And if it came up, and she was challenged for being a city girl who would never understand how small towns worked, she was going to tell them who she was.

She'd heard the argument a few times now and not just during the presentation. At the market, at the pawnshop. It was as if she'd come from the moon not Denver.

She'd been debating the issue on and off since the mess at the first presentation. But after today, after being with Mike and brainstorming about drawing on the other towns in the area, she decided it would be a plus for the townspeople to know that she knew what she was talking about from experience.

Okay, it would also be a thrill to see the shocked look on all their faces. But that would be a bonus. Nothing more.

THE MORNING'S CHORES had taken some time, given the chill in the air. Mike had brought the calves and their dams into the shed the night before, and this morning he'd strengthened their bedding with thick, fresh straw and fitted them all with jackets, even though the shed was well ventilated and had auxiliary heating. The extended summer weather had played havoc with the breeding timetables, and there were more newborns than normal.

Since the forecast had mentioned some heavy gusts, he'd rolled in two of the windbreaks for the cattle in the pens.

But once he'd finished, he'd taken the fastest shower on record and hightailed it to the motel.

Savannah was waiting near the entrance wearing a jacket and the Stetson he'd loaned her yesterday. Her hair was down around her shoulders and her jeans fit like a glove. He hoped she'd want to go for another horseback ride today, but he'd be satisfied with anything she wanted to do.

Before he could get out to open the truck door, she'd hopped in. "Hey."

"Hey, yourself. You seem well rested."

She laughed. "Not really. Just happy to be spending the day out…with you."

That certainly raised his spirits, and they'd already been high as a kite. "So, where to first?"

"Twin Creeks?"

"Good starting point. It's Sunday, but there should be a place to eat that's open."

"Oh, I was up early and hit the lobby breakfast and had the most amazing cinnamon roll."

Mike nodded. "I've had those before. From the diner. Many, many times, in fact." He waited until a trailer truck passed then drove onto Main Street, heading toward the highway. "I assume you have our itinerary planned out?"

"Yes. But I'm completely open to changes. You're much more knowledgeable about the area than I am."

"Not as much as you'd think. I know more about the route to Billings than I do the local towns. If you can even call some of them towns. So we'll discover them together."

"Great. And just so you know, I plan to buy souvenirs and any other kind of tchotchkes that I find on the way."

"Are you telling me I should've brought a trailer?"

"I'm not *that* bad," she said, laughing. "I haven't asked you about your morning. I saw there was a wind advisory on the news."

She'd noticed that? He was already in trouble with Savannah, knowing she loved her job and that she was most definitely going back to Denver soon, and she kept making things worse. In the entire time he and Ellen had been married, she'd never mentioned anything about the weather unless it affected her directly.

Rounding up calves in the dead of winter, wind howling and frostbite an imminent threat for man and beast? Nothing. Rain on a spring outing to a baseball game? Tragedy.

He drove on, stealing glances at Savannah every chance he could. Half the time, he caught her looking his way. He felt like a damn kid.

When she still seemed concerned about how the calves would fare with the bad weather, he ended up telling her about the precautions he'd taken.

"But they'll be okay with us away for the afternoon?"

"Oh, yeah. No worries there."

"I never thought I'd find cows so interesting. Do you have to replace the bedding every day?"

"Not at this stage. You don't have to, but I like to, especially when we don't have a full house. But when the majority of the heifers give birth, which is normally a little later in the season, not only do you need to change the straw every day but everything else, including whoever is assisting the birth. You get soaking wet, sometimes for hours, and there's no place to wash the slime off in the shed. Even if you can wash outside, it won't be with hot water."

She sat with that for a minute, drawing little thumb circles on her thigh. He forced himself to watch the traffic.

"You really do love ranching. You'd have to, to go through that year after year."

"Except for the mess, calving is the best time of year. It depends on the weather, of course, and how healthy the herd is, but if it's nice out, cutting the calves is one of the most cowboy things we do. Always on horseback, not using ATVs like some."

"Cutting the calves?"

"It's separating them out of the main herd so we can take care of them better."

"Exactly what I thought."

"Of course you did," he said. "We're coming into Twin Creeks now."

"There's nothing out there," she said. "Except that house up on the hill."

"Can't say I didn't warn you. But at least it's pretty this time of year."

"It is. I live in the downtown area of Denver. It's nice, and I do love the access to everything so close by…"

"For instance?"

"Restaurants. We've got a thriving culinary scene. Great chefs, outstanding farmers' markets. We've got the Denver Center for the Performing Arts, the Colorado Symphony, terrific museums. Then there's skiing and hiking. It's really a nice place."

"Sounds like it," he said, trying to be earnest. Naturally she'd like it there. Denver was a real city with things to do, places to go.

His experience of the world at large was like a postage stamp on an atlas. Billings was the metropolis of Montana, but he'd never had enough money or time to take advantage of it. And while he'd visited Denver, Las Vegas and central Florida, those had all been for auctions or quick trips to visit family that didn't include any sightseeing. When he'd played college ball, he'd traveled to other cities. But there again, he'd gone with the team and only for the games.

Yep, she'd been born in Blackfoot Falls, but they were from totally different worlds. She might be curious about the ranch, but he couldn't imagine her wanting to live on one. Listening to her questions, knowing she was genuinely interested in his answers made it easy to forget that not-so-small detail. He couldn't think about that, though, and ruin their last day together.

"In about twenty minutes, you're going to have a decision to make."

"What's that?" She folded her left leg underneath her right, squirming a little to adjust the seat belt so she could look at him more easily.

"Do we go to the diner, which amounts to a few seats at the drugstore counter and a very limited menu, the new barbecue joint or the drive-through?"

"Wow. What a selection."

"Consider wisely. There's every chance a wrong decision could color your entire experience of northwestern Montana."

She laughed, But his own attempt at a smile wasn't nearly as successful.

SAVANNAH FINISHED HER lunch at Uncle Walt's Barbecue, and Mike pushed away his plate, too. The restaurant was reasonably crowded, and it appeared that at least two tables were hosting tourists. He'd said hello to a couple of cowboys he recognized.

Although she'd spent a decent amount of time observing the people, the place and even the state of the restroom, all she'd wanted to do was talk to Mike. Everything about him drew her in. It was as if they'd known each other all their lives. It was kind of crazy, the way they got along.

"Are you going to get some dessert?" he asked.

She'd only had a salad, so she technically could, but after that huge cinnamon roll, she shouldn't. "Do you think those pies in the cooler are fresh or frozen?"

He leaned closer to her. "I have a surefire way of telling." He scooted his chair over. "You see the way the crust is crimped?"

She nodded, wondering if this was something his mother had taught him. "Yes?"

"It's nice," he said, then turned to look at the waitress who was standing behind Savannah. "Those pies fresh?"

Savannah gave him an evil look but was glad when the waitress, who had the highest little voice, said, "Yep. Made fresh every morning. In my opinion, the huckleberry is the best, although some folks really like the apple."

"I'll have a slice of the berry," Savannah said. "A small one, please." She turned to Mike. "Unless you want to share."

Mike grinned. "How about making it big and à la mode?"

The waitress nodded. "Sure thing."

Savannah kicked the heel of his boot. "That was sneaky. After we have the pie, which you have to eat most of, I'd like to walk down the street—go in, if anything's open."

"The only place open will be the gas-station shop."

"At least we can look in the windows. I've been meaning to ask. Are all the towns around here football crazy? I saw the banners and memorabilia for the Blackfoot Falls Bisons. And now it's the Twin Creeks Falcons. I should get a sweatshirt from both teams…for my collection."

"You're that into football?"

"Nope. Winters are freezing in Denver."

"It's a pity you couldn't be here for the big game."

"Big game? Gee, I'm not sure what you mean. Not like

there's a giant billboard advertising it on the way into town. Or fightin' words painted on half the windows and cars cheering on the Falcons. Or banners down the main drag or a big sign right behind you."

"Yeah," he said, grinning. "That game."

"Yesterday I noticed a few Bisons banners had replaced some Halloween decorations. Is this the end of the season or something?"

"Nope. See, any time the Bisons or Falcons go up against another town, it's a big hoopla. But playing each other? That's the worst."

"How so?"

"Some folks take the rivalry too far. I wouldn't be caught dead at the Watering Hole or the Full Moon during the week leading up to those games."

"That bad, huh?"

"After a little too much booze? You bet. Good thing everyone is afraid of Sadie."

Savannah grinned. "As well they should be."

"Amen to that."

"What about baseball? Same enthusiasm?"

"Not quite. Spring and summer are busy seasons for ranchers. But yeah, sports gets people out of the house. They tailgate a lot and gossip, of course, and more than a little betting goes on."

"Ah, right," she said, nodding. "I can see local sports would be popular."

"And don't forget rodeo. After all, this is cowboy country," he said, pitching his voice so low it broke on the end of the word.

Savannah laughed. She liked this man. So much. Too much.

"So, where to next?" he asked. "Greenville? Then swing by Munson?"

"You're the tour guide."

"Yeah, well, the whole thing should take us all of ten minutes. You think this town is small. Greenville has about eight hundred people. Half that for Munson."

"Greenville is much more spread out, though. Lots of medium-size ranches, and I read they also have a sizable wind farm."

"That wasn't there the last time I drove through town."

The pie arrived and it was delicious. When it was time to go, Mike wanted to pay, but she stopped that with a glare and her corporate credit card.

The walk turned out to be informative. The market was actually open, although it was smaller by half than the one in Blackfoot Falls and not very appealing. The hardware store was closed but had a lot of feed and lumber stacked outside. There was a pawnshop that mostly sold guns and fishing supplies and a thrift shop that opened three days a week.

Mike held the door open for her once they got back to the truck. "Feel like you've learned something?"

"Actually, yes." She waited until he climbed in before she continued. "They could do a lot more. Tourists love pawnshops and thrift stores. I wonder who owns the storefronts that are closed. Do you think they belong to the city?"

He started them on their way to Greenville. "Hard to say. I know of at least one private owner—Lawrence Peabody. He bought up quite a few properties. Grabbed them a few years back when prices hit rock bottom."

"Huh. Was he at the presentation?"

"Not that I noticed, but I heard he bought the old drive-through in Blackfoot Falls. Wants to turn it into a casual restaurant."

"That's excellent. I would've thought he'd be interested in hearing our recommendations."

"Sadie might not have mentioned it to him. Lawrence lives east of Twin Creeks." Mike paused. "He's not everyone's favorite person. And that's all I'll say."

"Ah." Savannah could tell Mike didn't care for the man either. "Anyway, one billboard on the highway could increase both Twin Creeks's and Blackfoot Falls's business significantly. And Lord knows the people around here don't seem to object to them," she said as they passed yet another billboard rallying the Falcons to obliterate the Bisons.

"Uncle Walt's should be advertising. I'm not saying it's the best barbecue I've ever eaten, but having another restaurant is a big improvement."

"We have to remember to tell Chip his ribs were much better," she said, and Mike smiled. "I just hope that Greenville and Munson have at least one unique attraction each. That's all they'd need to get things moving. And anything that draws people to the area will help Blackfoot Falls."

"I'm glad it was worth your while."

"Lunch with you was worth it all by itself. I wouldn't have minded if we did nothing else."

He smiled at her. "Me, too," he said, and reached for her hand.

It seemed like the most natural thing in the world for her to thread her fingers through his. "I really appreciate you spending your day chauffeuring me around."

"There's no place I'd rather be but right here."

Savannah bit her lip. "Will we have enough time to go to the cabin?"

"If that's what you want, absolutely."

"I wasn't sure this morning," she said. "But I want to see it now. Not sure I'm going to enjoy the visit, mind you."

Mike squeezed her hand. "You're an amazing woman, Savannah." Her breath caught as she realized it was because of him that she was willing to go see the cabin. Mike made

her feel safe, strong, empowered. In fact, Mike made her
a feel a lot of things.

Things she'd never felt before.

Chapter Fifteen

Mike was surprised at the growth of Greenville. Main Street had a couple new shops, replacing stores that had been closed up for years. A taxidermist with plenty of samples on display, an auto-parts store and a small café that wasn't open on Sunday and when it was, they only served breakfast and lunch. It looked nice and modern, at least from the window. Evidently, it was a good omen, and Savannah was enthusiastic about it.

The gas station had become more of a mini travel stop since Mike had last seen it. A small addition had expanded the little shop that offered snacks and souvenirs, mostly to do with Glacier National Park. But what made it a fun place to shop, according to Savannah, were the local goods, such as leather purses and jackets, handwoven rugs and baskets, even children's toys.

She bought a suede purse and a wooden train for her neighbor's son. She also spoke to the guy running the place. He told her they did a decent business, but there wasn't much of a push to get tourists. Which was a shame, in his opinion, because the area had some of the best trout fishing in the state, and great camping facilities.

Munson was just a step above the sleepy town Mike remembered from years ago. The gas station was smaller than the one in Greenville, though it boasted a shelf of local honey and homemade jams.

The conversation with the young fellow behind the register wasn't terribly illuminating, given that he was far more interested in the game on his tablet than in his customers.

As they drove out of town, Savannah remembered the dinosaur tracks. "Did you even see a sign for them?" she asked. "I didn't."

"No, I didn't either." He'd been a kid, but he was fairly certain they'd come to Munson on their field trip. "There's a campground up ahead. Let's stop."

"It looks new," she said as they got closer.

"I don't remember it being here before."

There were a surprising number of RVs parked, with more hookups available, and the grounds were well maintained. Mike drove toward a woman carrying a basket of clothes out of a building marked Laundry, passing a tower of signs pointing to local fishing spots and scenic lookouts.

"Well, damn, they sure don't have anything against signage. Maybe I'm wrong about the dinosaur tracks. Could be in Minersville."

"We'll just ask," Savannah said, already letting down her window.

The woman, who turned out to be the manager, greeted them with a friendly smile, and was more than happy to answer all their questions. Mike hadn't been wrong; the dinosaur tracks were located on the other side of town. But a strong gust of wind had brought the sign down last spring, and no one had put it back up.

Savannah thanked the woman then wrote down a few notes as Mike got them back on the highway. They had one more stop to make before they headed to her family's old cabin.

Turned out the movie people hadn't built a ghost town

like Mike had thought. Minersville *was* the ghost town. The place had been abandoned along with the boarded-up gold mine located to the east. It wasn't specifically for tourists, but since it had been used as a movie set the buildings were safe to walk through. Other than that, there were a few homes and small ranches in the area.

"How far is Minersville from Blackfoot Falls? Not your place but the town itself?" Savannah asked as they got under way.

"About fifty miles—an hour's drive on the highway."

"How about between Greensville and Minersville? Maybe forty minutes?"

"Yep, that's a fair estimate."

Savannah jotted down more notes. "If all the towns got together, I don't think it would take much work to turn Minersville into something touristy. It could be a nice day trip."

"If the county owns the buildings, I'm sure they'd be all for turning the place into a moneymaker."

"Hopefully," she said, closing the notebook and turning to stare out the window.

She was quiet after that. Not surprising. Seeing the cabin was sure to bring up a lot of old memories. He put some music on low, hoping it would make Savannah more comfortable.

"I'm sorry," she said fifteen minutes later.

"For what?"

"Being so moody. I thought this would be easier."

"I didn't imagine it would be. If nothing else, it's going to remind you of the day you left. Not a simple thing to process."

"No. But, you'd think after all the work I've done, turning my life into something I'm proud of…" Sighing, she laid her head back. "I don't know. I'm probably overthinking this. Getting through college while working full-time was hard. This will be a piece of cake."

"Hey, give yourself a break. If you're feeling too edgy, maybe this isn't a good idea."

She just shrugged. "My mom would think I'm nuts coming back here."

"Where does she live now?"

"Kentucky, of all places. Her husband's hometown. She met him two years after we moved to Denver. Richard had just gotten out of the service. He's a good man."

"Did he adopt you?"

"What?" She seemed startled, but then she nodded. "Oh, no. James *is* his last name, but after the scandal, and since my dad didn't seem to give a fig about me anyway, I begged to have it changed."

"You visit them much?"

"Not really. They left my freshman year at Boulder. He works as a plumber, but he has a boy with special needs. Turns out Mom's very good with him. She's incredibly patient, and she's done so much research, making his life as vibrant as possible."

"That's great."

"It is. It's helped me, too. Watching her with Tim. And with Richard. I'm glad they're happy. But I must admit, I haven't made total peace with her yet. My therapist said there's no time limit and no expectations, but I want to. I want her to see me as the person I am now. It's only fair that I return the sentiment."

"I don't know if fairness has a great deal to do with the parent-child relationship. My mother had a hard time with my sister when she was a teenager. It seemed like they were always mad at one another, and they can still rub each other the wrong way. The grandkids help a lot, though."

"My mother hints about my prospects, having grandchildren and how I'd love Kentucky." She lowered her voice. "I really wouldn't."

He smiled, kind of hoping she'd say more about her view on having kids. Instead, they lapsed into silence until he took the turnoff that led to the cabin. Savannah tensed. The way she was rubbing her hands was pure nerves. If she said the word, he'd turn around in a second.

Chapter Sixteen

The cabin was both smaller and larger than in her head. The tree she'd planted, only a sapling on her fifth birthday, was now over twenty feet high. The leaves had turned a dark burgundy, most of them blanketing the ground, providing cover for the little creatures she'd gotten to know so well. She climbed out of the truck, heard Mike's door slam and then felt him next to her. But she didn't look away from the earth.

"When I was small, I used to build towns for the insects. I'd lie in the dirt, where there were worms, beetles, ants. I spent hours digging them pathways and filling tiny ponds with water. I even made hills and little houses out of mud and twigs."

"That sounds like fun. I didn't know girls did those kinds of things."

She looked at him and laughed. "Well, I can't speak for *all* girls. And honestly, right now, it's all I can do not to shudder just thinking about anything crawling over me." She paused for a moment. "My mom must've liked bugs, too. She taught me all their common names first, but by the time I was twelve, I'd learned their scientific names, order, family, genus and species."

Mike's eyebrows rose.

"She was an exceptional teacher. And seamstress. She'd

made me a cloth bag to wear over my shoulder, complete with notebook, pencils, highlighters and a booklet called *Discover Entomology...*" Her throat had tightened with an unexpected lump, and she swallowed until it disappeared. "I read it so often, she replaced it twice."

Crouching, she cleared away some of the leaves. Of course, there was no trace of her childhood village, but the fond memory would always stay with her. She looked up and accepted Mike's outstretched hand.

He pulled her to her feet, and she stood close as they looked into each other's eyes. "How are you doing, Savannah?"

"Not too bad."

"I expect it'll come in waves."

Nodding, she released his hand then followed his gaze to the cabin.

"I told you it wasn't going to be in great shape," he said.

"Still has four walls and most of a roof. Even the chimney is standing—more or less."

"Listen," he said, "last time I was here was several years ago, when I saw smoke out this way. Turned out some kids had tried to use the fireplace and nearly killed themselves in the process. The smoke didn't vent, and they were drunk or stoned. Everyone came out of it alive, although they'd broken the lock and a couple windows. I'm sorry I didn't warn you before now."

Nodding, her gaze strayed to the front door and her pulse quickened. Funny how she'd assumed her visit to the creek was enough of a pilgrimage. Now it was clear she'd needed to come to the cabin. Regardless of what it looked like inside or out.

"I don't know why I'm shaking," she said, staring at her hands. "There's nothing in there that's going to hurt me."

"We don't have to stay," Mike said, sticking close.

"Thanks, but I want to finish this."

"Why don't I go in first, just in case."

"In case of what?"

"It was a real mess the last time. I don't want you to see it like that."

"For all I know, someone else's mess might be just the ticket."

He nodded and waited.

As with most things in life, the first step was the hardest. After that, she looked at the cabin as if it were someone else's. Her gaze caught on little things. A glass shard in the sunlight as she reached the door. A footprint, big, where the doorknob dangled. A squeak she didn't recognize as she pushed in.

Of course, it was dark. Even back when she was a kid, the trees around them had blocked out a lot of the sun. But now, with the odd angle of the light, the air was ghostly with dust particles and wisps of webs.

Some furniture was still in the main room. The kitchen sink was broken and the counters were disgusting and battered. Her gaze kept returning to the dining-room table. It had never been anything special, just some wood slapped together by her grandfather. She remembered him, even though he'd died when she was four. He'd had wild hair, and he had made her laugh.

"Oh, for heaven's… It still has the phone book underneath the leg," she said. "My grandfather was a terrible carpenter. He never measured anything—that leg was an inch shorter than the rest."

"That's one way to fix it." Mike was grinning again, his arms folded across his chest, his back straight and strong. As if he were a guardian instead of a…

What was Mike? A friend? An ally? Yes, but maybe

more? While she wasn't exactly sure what they were, she was awfully grateful for him.

Two chairs pulled over close to the fireplace were still on four legs, although she wouldn't dare sit on them. The old, ugly couch her father had picked up from a yard sale hadn't ever smelled great, but now the old lumps had gotten much larger. Perhaps there was a colony inside it now. Squirrels? Mice?

Mike had been right about the trash. Beer bottles, cigarette butts and empty wine bottles littered the floor. There was a flannel shirt in the corner, covered with dust. Strangely, seeing it like this did help. Her mother had always made sure the house was spotless.

"I don't think I need to see the bathroom," she said as she moved into the back part of the cabin. The bathroom was between her parents' bedroom and her own. It had been terrible placement. With their plasterboard walls she'd heard most everything.

She'd saved up for months to buy a pair of headphones, which didn't even work with the old radio she had. So she'd stuffed cotton in her ears and put the headphones over that.

"This was Mom's," Savannah said, wandering into her mother's bedroom first.

The bed had been smashed, and the old headboard was missing completely. The dresser was in even worse shape. What had happened in this room? Nothing she wanted to know about.

"Whoa," Mike said, grasping her arms as she ran into him.

"Sorry, I didn't realize you were so close."

"It's all right," he said, looking intently into her eyes. "You still okay?"

"Yeah. Pretty much. Just, some memories are better than others."

"Understandable. I have a few that make me cringe, and I doubt they're going away anytime soon."

Savannah smiled at the face he made. Clearly he hadn't said that just to make her feel better. Then she saw the old dry-erase board her mother had used for math equations.

"I can't believe she left this behind," Savannah said, picking it up and dusting it off. "Although she must've had a dozen of them. With today's tech, this seems almost archaic."

"Maybe, but I bet it did the job."

"Oh, yeah." She wondered if the pens were still around. But in this mess, she wasn't about to search for them. "Mom didn't follow a regular curriculum, which I didn't understand until much later. She made sure she followed the Montana laws for homeschooling, but she was much more interested in pursuing the things I was excited about. Not an easy task, since I was voraciously curious. We'd planned on getting a used RV and traveling across the country to visit historical sites."

"That would've been something."

"Yep. We never had the money, and then I begged her to let me go to the high school. But I learned a lot from her. I'm sure I got more from her teaching than I ever would have from a traditional education."

"Was she accredited?"

"No. All she was allowed to do was homeschool. But with the wisdom of age, I've realized she's a smart woman. She could've done much more with her life." Savannah shrugged. "If she hadn't married my dad."

"I'm glad you had a good education. It's certainly paid off."

"It has," she said, relieved to leave her mother's room but still a little wary of looking inside her own. Her room had been her sanctuary. "I'm glad you're with me. And I promise I'm almost ready to go."

He shook his head. "Take as much time as you need."

The door squeaked. It always had, but now it sounded more like a scary-movie sound effect. She peeked inside, and her gaze stopped at her bed. It was messed up. Thinking about who might've used it since wasn't a good idea, so she focused on how tiny it was. A twin bed. Maybe smaller than that, she wasn't sure.

She'd forgotten about the poster above it. The old thing was hanging by one nail, but she knew the picture well. It was a shot of Glacier National Park, the snowcapped mountains above their mirror image in a pristine lake.

She'd been there once. "We had a TV, but it wasn't connected to an antenna," she said. "We did have a VCR and seventeen tapes. I watched them all dozens and dozens of times."

"What was your favorite?"

"*The Parent Trap.* And I loved *Armageddon.* I've got the DVDs but I haven't seen them in a while. With work, I don't have time, and when I do I prefer going to a theater."

"I do, too. Kalispell has two nice movie stadiums now."

Her eyes closed as she wondered what life would have been like if her mother had never…if they'd never left. Would she and Mike have found each other? Would they have gone to the movies in Kalispell? Probably not. She would have done everything in her power to get out of Blackfoot Falls on her eighteenth birthday, if not before.

She turned back to the room. Her window had been broken by a rock that sat on the floor. "I used to crawl out that window at night, get into my sleeping bag and watch the stars. Then at first light, I'd go into the woods and try to sneak up on the deer."

Mike smiled. "How did that work out?"

"Oh, they saw me coming a mile away. Although… I actually became friends with one, a young doe. I fed her apples. But she left."

"No pets?"

"No pets. My father was allergic." The mix of memories and emotions were beginning to overwhelm her. She needed time to process. "You know what? I think I'm ready to go. Is that all right?"

"That's fine. Come on." Mike held the door for her, his arm outstretched.

They took the short walk to the truck in silence. Mike stayed a step behind her, his way of giving her a modicum of privacy.

"Savannah?"

She started to turn to him then realized he'd opened the passenger door and was waiting for her.

The concern in his dark eyes tugged at her heart. "Thank you," she said.

"I'm sorry. I wish this could've been easier for you." His brows lifted in mild surprise when she slid her arms around his neck.

"It wasn't easy, but it was good. You did that, you made it painless."

"I don't see how." He put his hands on her waist but didn't try to pull her closer.

"By coming with me. By being a shoulder for me to lean on. By not judging me. I could keep going…"

"Savannah, you did all the heavy lifting. You prepared yourself for this day by going to therapy, which I know nothing about except that you had to be brave as hell. As for judging you? Why would I do that? I feel like a wimp next to you."

She laughed then melted a little at the smile he gave her. "You know what?" she said, pressing closer.

"What?"

"Even if this entire trip had ended up a disaster, it would have been worth every minute just so I could get to know you."

He let go of her waist and put his arms around her. "I had a similar thought...although the circumstances were just a little different in my version."

"Just a little?" She tilted her head back.

"Yeah, no disaster involved." He kissed the tip of her nose.

Savannah let out a silly laugh, startling herself. "I giggled."

"You did."

"I never giggle."

"Can't say that anymore."

"Bet you'd let me get away with it."

Mike smiled. "Bet you're right," he said, and lowered his mouth to hers.

Chapter Seventeen

After they'd polished off the leftover ribs and potato salad, Savannah carried their plates to the sink while Mike started a pot of coffee. "Are you sure you don't want to take me back to town now? I know you have to get up early tomorrow."

"Having second thoughts?"

"No, of course not." She felt him come up behind her, and she held her breath as he reached around her for a box of filters. "Wait, second thoughts about what?"

Mike's husky chuckle tickled her ear. "Hanging out for a while."

"Right. That's what I figured."

He lingered, even though he had the box of filters in hand. His lips brushed the side of her neck. "We won't do anything you don't want to do," he whispered, pausing to nip at her earlobe. "I promised and I meant it."

Savannah couldn't help the small shiver that worked its way down her spine. "I should never have admitted I'm ticklish there."

"You didn't admit anything," he said with a laugh, and leaned back. "I found out for myself."

"Technically, I guess that's true."

"Technically?"

"That's right." She elbowed him. "You're in the way. Unless you don't want these plates to go in the dishwasher."

"Leave everything in the sink. I'll take care of it later."

Shaking her head, she shooed him away. "Let's just clean up now. That coffee is half decaf, right? I still need to work on my presentation, but I don't want to stay up all night."

"Half decaf, as requested."

After opening the dishwasher, she felt his eyes on her and she looked up. "Why are you staring at me?"

"I'm trying to decide if that was a hint."

She had to think back a second. "No, I want to stay, as long as I'm not interfering with any chores you need to do. I understand ranching is a 24/7 job." She straightened and dried her hands. "Not to belabor the point, but I really hope you understand I won't be spending the night."

"I do. I fully intend to take you back to town the minute you tell me you want to go."

Savannah arched a brow, suspicious of his careful wording. "And I don't want you trying to convince me to stay overnight either."

"Won't happen."

"Not even if I convince *myself* to stay."

Mike frowned. "Run that by me again."

"Look, it would be too easy to just—I don't need the temptation, okay? Despite all the kissing we've been doing and will probably continue to—" She laughed at his instant grin.

He abandoned the coffeepot and, holding her gaze, he crossed the kitchen and pulled her into his arms. "You mean like this?" he murmured, and brushed his mouth across hers.

Before she could respond, his tongue traced the curve of her jaw to the sensitive spot below her ear.

"See?" she whispered, tilting her head to give him better access. "You said you wouldn't tempt me."

"I promised I wouldn't try to convince you, and I won't." He took a light nip then soothed the area with his tongue.

She let her head fall back, and her body arched into his embrace as his warm lips paid homage to her throat. "I should've been more specific," she whimpered.

"You're safe," he said, his hot, moist breath stirring her hair. "I'll get you back to town tonight, even if I have to carry you kicking and screaming to my truck."

He took Savannah's soft gasp as an invitation and slipped his tongue between her parted lips. His hands were warm and strong on her back, and she was weakening with every passing second. Another minute and her resolve would be nothing but mush.

She shifted, just a little, not sure if she wanted the kiss to end or heat up. It was Mike who finally retreated. One second he was kissing her and the next he lowered his arms and stepped back. And she was pretty sure she knew why. He was hard, and her sudden movement probably hadn't helped.

"Better finish making the coffee," he said, running a hand over his face and exhaling.

Feeling oddly bereft, Savannah swallowed and nodded. "You still feel like watching a movie?" she asked, fully prepared for him to suggest they call it quits for the evening.

"Sure. I'll even try to behave." He smiled wryly. "No promises, though."

That eased her anxiety. But damn, she'd better figure out what exactly she wanted and stick to it. Really, would it be so terrible to spend the night with him? She wasn't committed to Porter. And for goodness sake, she hadn't had sex in forever.

Mike had returned to his task, while she just stood there, staring at nothing and thinking way too much.

"I need to ask," Mike said suddenly. "Are you seeing anyone?"

Savannah should've expected the question. In fact, she'd waited for it a few times yesterday. "Kind of." She shook her head. "Not really." Yeah, that didn't sound evasive at all. Jeez.

"How long?"

"Two months." She hoped his frown didn't mean he thought she was lying. "We've only gone out a few times."

"That's all?"

"We haven't had sex," she blurted, blushing like crazy when the words tumbled out. "Oh, God. That was a terrible thing to—" She sighed at his slow smile. "I know, I know, way too much information."

"No, actually, I'm relieved, so—" he shrugged "—thanks."

"Honestly, it's not really going anywhere. Porter's got some personal issues to work out, so it's just been a couple of dinners and drinks. And I've already decided—"

Mike had tensed. It was a slight shift in his expression, his posture, but real nevertheless. "You don't need to explain anything to me."

"I just didn't want you to think I played loose—or that I'm anything like my mother." Her stomach churned. Why hadn't she just shut up? "I didn't mean that. Not like it sounded."

Except she did, and she turned back to loading the dishwasher before he could see the ugly truth in her eyes.

"Hey." He caught her arm and gently pulled her back around to face him. "The thought never crossed my mind."

"Just for the record, my mom isn't like that anymore. That was a crappy thing for me to say."

"I knew what you meant. And certainly no one would

blame you for being touchy." He traced the skin over her cheekbone with his thumb. Once, twice. Then again. "This is torture."

"What is?"

"Touching you."

A warm, giddy sensation took over her senses and erased any lingering doubt. "Then don't do it," she said, trying to control a grin.

His low, intimate laugh made her shiver with anticipation. Looping her arms around his neck, she pushed up on her toes. Her lips barely reached his, but anyway pressing herself against his hard body elicited a much better response.

A wickedly deep groan echoed from the back of his throat. She heard the pounding of her own heart, felt the beating of his against her breasts as he claimed her with an openmouthed kiss. His tongue swept inside, finding and stroking hers until her knees started to weaken.

His hand slipped down to the curve of her backside and, exerting a light pressure, he urged her more firmly against him. Sanity had fled with the touch of his hand and the taste of his mouth. Her resolve to stay out of his bed was following close behind.

She doubted Porter could ever make her feel like this.

The callous thought cooled her off some. She wasn't doing anything wrong, but she was so tempted...

Mike evidently noticed the change in her mood. He broke the kiss and stepped back, clearing his throat. "Okay. Coffee."

Savannah nodded and as he turned toward the coffee maker, she glimpsed the bulge in his jeans.

"Why don't you go choose a DVD while I finish up?" he said, his voice hoarse. "Assuming you still want to stay."

"I do."

"Good. I'll join you in a minute." She was glad he kept his back to her, since she needed some time to cool down herself.

Somehow she made it to the couch. Just as she sank down onto the cushion, she remembered she was supposed to pick out a movie. Even if she managed to stand, she wasn't sure she'd be able to control her impulses. But if she gave in and slept with Mike, what would tomorrow be like? Seeing everyone from town. Them seeing her. Would it be written all over their faces? Would it embarrass him? Make her seem less professional?

She shouldn't do it, that was all. She needed to control herself, at least until after her work here was finished.

THE COFFEE DRIPPED, the sizzle on the hot surface below the pot an excellent representation of Mike's thoughts. Her company was called Porter Burke International. The chances of their being another Porter at that company were pretty much nil. The man Savannah had spoken to yesterday was Porter Burke. Her boss.

She had to know that taking up with her boss was a dicey move. She'd put the career she said she loved at risk. Savannah was smart. Clever. Intuitive. It didn't sound like something she'd do.

Did those kinds of relationships ever work out? Maybe. He'd never worked in an office environment, and just because common knowledge said it was a stupid move didn't mean all that much.

Maybe he'd misunderstood, but he didn't think so.

Instead of going to the den, he got a package of microwave popcorn from the pantry and popped it then put it in the ceramic bowl he'd bought for his father about twenty birthdays ago. It said Dad's Popcorn—Hands Off on the side. His dad took that inscription to heart. Using it was a guilty pleasure when his folks were in Florida.

The coffee was ready, so he filled a cup for her and took out a soda for himself. Just in case, he added another soda to the tray and walked it all out to the living room.

The TV was off, and Savannah was sitting on the edge of the sofa, staring at the dark screen.

"What did you pick?"

His voice startled her, making her head jerk. "Sorry, I forgot. I'll go look now. Is that popcorn I smell?"

"Yeah. Well, you know. Movie." He put the tray on the coffee table as she stood.

When she came back to the couch, she was holding his copy of *Moonrise Kingdom*. "This okay?"

"Yeah, great."

The movie was running a minute later, but Mike wasn't paying much attention. He was too busy staring at her hand as she swiped popcorn from the bowl. Her fingers were long and elegant with neatly trimmed nails.

"Did I mention," she said, right in the middle of Bill Murray's dialogue, "that I'm putting in for a week of vacation starting on Tuesday?"

"Vacation." The popcorn in his hand dribbled back into the bowl. "Here?"

She grinned at him. "Yep." She flicked a kernel into her mouth."

"Seriously?"

Her smile didn't waver. "And I'll tell you something else I've decided."

"What's that?" he asked, hoping like hell it was to spend the night with him.

"If anyone makes a comment about me not understanding small towns, I'm going to tell them who I am."

It felt like a sucker punch. Her joy at her plan was painfully obvious, and so, so misguided. But he needed to be careful. Not make her paranoid.

"What?" she said, her smile dimming.

"That's a big turnaround. I'm not sure it's going to do you any favors."

"What do you mean?"

He let go of his held breath. "You remember what those people were like at the last presentation. They haven't suddenly become more rational."

"True. But it should help if they know I understand."

"Didn't you tell me you've lived in Denver since you left here?"

Her eyes narrowed. "Yes."

"Someone's bound to mention you were only fourteen when you left, and you were hardly ever in town."

"That just means my world was even smaller."

God, he hated this. "I don't know, there's a difference between living an isolated childhood and growing up in a small town."

"You think they're right, don't you? I don't understand the culture." She visibly swallowed and then seemed to deflate before his eyes. "Or is this about my mom? It is, isn't it? They'll blame me—"

"No. That's not what I'm saying." He paused, afraid he'd unintentionally brought them down this rocky path. No, she didn't understand the small town mind-set, but the conversation had veered to something more personal. "Naturally, there will be a few who'll pick on anything to complain about. Doubly so when there's even a minor threat of change in the air."

"I don't believe it," she said, looking away from him. "You said it was all on my mother, and that I had nothing to be ashamed of."

"You don't. Believe me, you don't. But you've seen what some of the older folks around here are like…"

When she turned to face him, she looked bleak. "How do you stand it, then? These people who are so stubborn, or is it just willful? I never wanted to think that small towns meant small minds."

"That's not fair," he said. "We're talking about a few vocal individuals. You said yesterday the folks you met at the diner had been smart and savvy."

"No use talking about it. I don't even know if I'll say anything."

He wanted to put his arms around her. Help her see that he was trying to do her a favor. "Look, anyplace you live is a trade-off. My family had a rough go after the economy tanked. The ranch wasn't making enough to pay the bills. But I'm good with carpentry, and the people in town know it. They hired me, even though some weren't all that much better off. They had me doing remodels and repairs and everything in between. And some of those people were part of the group that was giving you so much grief. Mostly, they're all good-hearted, kind folks and believe me, they're in the majority."

She stood up, making it clear his message hadn't been welcome.

"May I just add one more thing?" he said. "I'm not saying don't do it, but I think tomorrow's forum is a lousy time."

She blinked and looked away.

Hell, maybe he should've used the termob mentality," since that was what he was thinking. But he was battling more than Savannah's disappointment. What she'd said about the town made it very clear that she would never want to live here again. Until now, he hadn't realized he'd subconsciously held on to a small hope she might, once the dust settled.

More than that, he realized with a sinking feeling, she hadn't let go of the past. She was still looking for validation from the outside. How else to explain such a sensible woman dating her boss? He could ruin her, and that hadn't scared her off?

And now she wanted to prove herself to the town that hadn't given one thought to the child who was thrown out with the bathwater. It wasn't enough that she was great at her job or that she was offering something tangible that could help Blackfoot Falls and everyone in it.

"I need to do some thinking," she said with a strained smile. "Would you mind taking me back to the motel?"

Chapter Eighteen

The next morning Savannah turned on her laptop as she sipped her coffee. First, she checked her calendar to make sure she had nothing pressing to do this week. If she'd ever needed a vacation, it was now.

Sometime around midnight, she'd finally made peace with what Mike had told her. She understood that he was just playing devil's advocate, and that he had her best interest at heart. Fortunately, they hadn't parted on a bad note, and she was reasonably certain he'd still welcome her hanging out with him for a week.

Also, she needed him to know that she appreciated his efforts. Though she was still prepared to reveal who she was if the occasion demanded it, knowing she could take whatever heat came her way. After visiting the cabin, she'd never felt stronger.

Next, Savannah called the office. It was already ten fifteen and she hoped her supervisor wasn't in a meeting. Jeanine was also the Denver regional manager, and she was going to faint when Savannah asked her for vacation time.

Jeanine answered on the third ring.

"Hey," Savannah said. "Are you sitting down?"

"Uh-oh. Tell me you're not about to blow up my Monday."

"I don't think so," Savannah said, grinning and picturing the older woman, who'd also been her mentor, juggling the phone and a mug of strong coffee.

"I got your email. You must still be in—what is it—Blackfoot Falls?"

"I am, but I should be finished by midafternoon. Listen, I checked my calendar and I don't have anything major scheduled. Can you spare me for a week? I want to take some vacation."

After a brief silence, Jeanine said, "I hope no one died."

"I almost killed Ron, but no, not that I'm aware of."

Jeanine chuckled. "He was asking about you a while ago."

"I will say he felt badly leaving me to finish up. But that was just fine with me. Anyway, vacation time?"

"I don't see a problem. We're covered, although Porter is coming next Monday so you might want to be up to speed on all your accounts by then."

Savannah frowned. "Isn't he in Paris for meetings?" She knew he was because she'd spoken to him earlier—right while she was in the middle of a juicy daydream about Mike. And Porter hadn't mentioned anything about going to Denver.

"According to his assistant, he's going to Milan for a few days, then flying here before returning to Dallas."

"Did she say why?"

"She didn't know." Jeanine paused. "I don't think either of us is getting fired."

It was a joke, so Savannah laughed, even though she didn't feel like it.

"Hey, I've got to run, but yes, absolutely, take vacation. Hell, with all the hours you work, I should consider it comp time."

Ten minutes ago Savannah would've loved that idea. It meant she could sock more time away to visit Mike later down the road. But it really bothered her that Porter hadn't said anything about Denver. Anyway, she wanted to see him in person to break things off, so the timing was great.

They disconnected, and Savannah bounced right back to dividing her thoughts between Mike and the presentation. His reservations about her identifying herself still gave her pause. She liked him twice as much for caring about her like this, so she'd decided not to identify herself. If necessary, she'd just tell them she came from a small town. After all, this wasn't about proving anything. Besides, she was a professional, and the job had to come first.

Mostly, though, she couldn't wait to tell him she'd gotten her vacation time. Maybe they could go up to Glacier National Park and to the movies in Kalispell. Okay, she had to concentrate on work right now. But she couldn't wait until after the presentation. She picked up her cell again and typed.

Guess who has a week of vacation starting tomorrow!

She'd barely returned to reviewing her notes when he texted back.

I'm all yours!

"OH, FOR CRYING out loud…" Sadie was facing the door, watching people stream into the room. "What the hell is he doing here?"

Savannah looked up from her laptop, though she had no idea who Sadie was talking about. It could've been any one of the sourpusses standing along the back wall. Some she recognized from Friday's presentation, mostly because they'd caused disruptions. No sign of Mike yet. But he'd show up.

She studied the room. Something wasn't right. "Sadie? I think we're missing a row of chairs."

"No, we aren't. I had them removed. If those old coots want to whine like a bunch of crybabies, let them do it standing up."

Savannah bit back a laugh. She was about to point out that the people who *should* be attending could end up without a seat, but then she saw that Sadie had taken that into account. The first three rows up front had been tagged with reserved signs, which said City Council Members and Merchants Only.

She pitied the first person to ignore the edict.

"We have five minutes. Kylie called to say she might be late." Sadie's gaze swept the crowded room. "Most of the other shopkeepers are here." Sadie moved in closer and leaned down, lowering her voice. "The woman at the end of the front row? That's Thelma Parsons, the council member I told you about. She's read your report, and don't be surprised when she whines about every little thing. Some folks think she's not all there," Sadie said, tapping her temple. "Feel free to ignore her. That's what we all try to do. Once you're ready to begin, I say we lock the doors."

Savannah half wished Sadie wasn't joking. "Hey, if I thought it would do any good…" She spotted Mike entering and couldn't help smiling.

"I'm curious," Sadie said. "Did you two already know each other before last week?"

Snapping to attention, she dragged her gaze away from Mike. "Not really," she said, which wasn't an outright lie. She met Sadie's eyes and decided to take a chance. "I used to live here. Not in town but out near the Burnetts' place."

Sadie's eyes widened. "No kidding."

"I was just a kid, though. Mike and I used to wave to each other, that's all." Savannah felt as if her heart might beat out of her chest. If she was this nervous telling Sadie, then maybe she wasn't ready to out herself to everyone.

"Huh." Sadie's brows lowered as she tried to solve the puzzle. "I must've known your folks—"

Savannah's stomach tightened and when her phone buzzed, she jumped on it. "Excuse me," she said. It was only a text, but she was thankful for the interruption.

Oh, cripes, what did Ron want? He'd texted and called twice already. Well, he'd just have to wait until after the presentation. What could be that urgent?

"ALL RIGHT, ALL RIGHT, everybody sit down or stand up against the back and shut up."

Sadie's voice filled the room as completely as the attendees. Savannah wasn't surprised. As far as she was concerned, Sadie should be in charge of all meetings, including the ones at her company.

"I can't stand up the whole damn time!"

"Well, then, Avery, go on home," Sadie said. "No reason for you to be here anyway."

"Hey, I got my rights."

"You have the right to be quiet. All of you have that right to remain silent through the presentation. We're not having a circus like last week. I mean it. There will be time to ask questions afterward. If you don't like the rules, bring it up at the next council meeting. If you don't keep to the rules, you'll be escorted out."

"I'll forget what my questions are by then."

Savannah recognized that old codger standing in the back. She wouldn't have minded if he'd forgotten to attend.

"I've got notepads and pencils for anyone who has a question. Mallory, do me a favor, help me pass these to anyone who wants one."

"I don't want no paper and pencil."

"Then don't ask questions, Jasper. It's up to you," Sadie said, smiling.

The mumbles that went through the crowd came in a wave from the back forward, but they mostly stopped before the folks in the reserved seats. Savannah wasn't going to begin until Sadie had everything quiet, but her Power-Point presentation was ready and her notes were in order, although she probably wouldn't have to look at them. The only thing she had to remember was to not stare at Mike through the whole thing.

After Mallory sat down, Sadie quieted the room in her signature take-no-prisoners way then introduced Savannah, finishing with a reminder that anyone who stepped out of line would step out the door.

"Thank you, Mayor," Savannah said, clicking to the first PowerPoint slide, which showed the town's logo. "In the interest of full disclosure, I want you all to know that I ran into some of the town merchants at the diner on Saturday, and we had a nice visit."

"Those weren't the only people you ran into," came a snarky voice from the rowdy section.

A couple of people turned around and looked at Mike. But they were all discouraged by Sadie's immediate rise, and her point directly at the one who'd spoken. "Earl, you do that again, and you're out."

Savannah continued as if nothing had happened. "I'll begin with a brief recap of our meeting on Friday, and then I'll get to the heart of what my colleagues and I discovered about your charming town, and how to not only increase revenue for all the local businesses but to make Blackfoot Falls a valued destination for anyone who wants to work or live in northwestern Montana."

As she went through the opening slides and gave her recap, the crowd was a little restless but mostly polite. Two more remarks were made, one by a woman and another by Earl, though he cut himself off when Sadie rose.

After the group chuckle was over, Savannah began the presentation in earnest. "I'm a firm believer that a town that works together can create great opportunities for themselves, their families and their community. The first thing we spoke about on Friday was the town's lack of proper signage. However we didn't discuss the solution. The first one is obvious—more signs.

"In conjunction with that, a visitor information center or welcoming committee would do very well. By that I mean a group of three or four community members getting together to figure out how best to direct folks to the local sights, the places to eat or where to stay, and how they can make the most out of their visit to Blackfoot Falls. That would include finding other interesting sights in the area, like the dinosaur tracks in Munson, the great fishing in Greenville and the Minersville ghost town."

"We're paying you to add income to our pockets, not our rivals'."

All Sadie had to do was stand up, and the miscreant shrank back into his seat.

"They're rivals in sporting events, yes, but none of these small towns, including yours, have enough unique experiences and shops to draw tourists by themselves, but by working together, you can all benefit greatly. You've got the advantage of being on the way to Glacier National Park. Why let people continue to pass Blackfoot Falls? It's a shame to send all that money to Kalispell and the park when some could be staying here.

"Together, you can also encourage new businesses to come and open their doors. Look how well the Full Moon has done. The Cake Whisperer. The new motel. They're all thriving and could do even better. I'd love to see all the town merchants join forces for a Facebook page, in addition to other joint social media efforts. Remember how well that's worked out for the Sundance ranch. All of that can be yours for very little capital, especially if—"

"We don't want new residents. We're happy just the way we are." The speaker was a middle-aged woman Savannah didn't recognize.

Then someone else from the crowd stood. "It all sounds great, but we're already working as hard as we can. You know what it takes to make money off a working ranch?"

The next person to rise was Thelma, and Savannah prepared for a deluge of negativity.

"You can't be serious. I mean, sure, we can use more signs, no complaints there, but why would we want all the trouble that comes with the internet? Stalkers and porn, that's what's on there. No decent people go on that internet."

"That's nonsense, Thelma," Sadie said, getting to her feet. "Just because you don't know how to navigate in the twenty-first century doesn't mean the rest of the town has to stay in the past."

Savannah clicked to the next slide, which pictured Safe Haven animal sanctuary. "You have so much to offer here," she said, making her voice the loudest in the room. "Like this amazing shelter for neglected and abandoned animals. People would love to visit and see the good work that goes on there. Maybe you could team up with the folks there and add a petting zoo. Families would eat that up.

"You also have great hiking, and trails for horseback riding and for ATVs. Possibly snowmobiles in the winter. And what a jackpot in movie sets you have. Does anyone have a list linking the sets to the movies?" She paused, though she knew the answer.

Most of the audience just stared blankly.

"These are great ideas, people." Rachel, from the Sundance, stood. "All of us could benefit. The local stores need every bit of help they can get. And we could use a few more motels and B & Bs, maybe even a campground. I bet we could draw more events like rodeos, if the fans weren't forced to drive to Kalispell for accommodations."

"I agree." Alice rose. "Listening to all this, I'm much more enthusiastic about opening my B & B. Sounds like we can all make some money. Tourists are a great way to let a lot of us older folks retire in comfort."

Just as Savannah was going to add her two cents, Jasper shouted everyone down. "The real problem is that some fancy Denver company and Miz James don't know the first thing about small towns. We'll lose every damn thing we hold special if we let her talk us into this carnival sideshow."

"Sir…" Savannah held up a hand. "I understand your concern. I really do. I happen to come from a small town, myself—"

"Like hell." Snorting, Jasper gave her a disdainful look. "You'd lie about anything to sell us a bunch of your malarkey…"

That did it. The whole crowd was devolving into chaos, and she had to get everyone back on track. Now. "Excuse me," she said. "I'm not a liar. I do know what small towns are like. In fact, I know what *this* small town is like, because I lived here for fourteen years."

"What?" Jasper's bewildered frown narrowed to a glare. "I don't know you and I've lived here all my life."

"My name is James now, but it used to be Riley."

At that, a collective gasp went up, although a few folks just looked confused.

"Are you Francine's daughter?" someone asked, the voice steeped in disbelief.

And then… Thelma raged to her feet. "How dare you step one foot in this town. You and your no-good family disgraced the name of Blackfoot Falls and every person who lived here. Your whore of a mother lured my husband away from me, and got him fired on top of it."

Sadie had stood up and was saying something, but the woman overrode her.

"He left town with no references because of you and your kind. The whole school almost crumbled because of you. We were made fools of, all of us." Thelma's eyes blazed. "You think you can waltz back in here like you aren't a taint upon the name of everything we hold holy and good?"

Savannah's breath had left her in a rush, and all the blood in her body turned to ice in her veins. Was that actually Mr. Jenkins's wife? Oh, God, why hadn't Mike warned her? She looked at him, but that made half the people now standing turn to stare right at him, too.

Rachel shot up from her seat and started telling everyone to settle down. Mallory tried to help, but chaos ruled. Even Sadie couldn't get them to all be quiet, and Savannah had to sit down before she fell to her knees.

Chapter Nineteen

Mike's first instinct was to rush to Savannah's side. But he quickly decided he would be of more use defusing the situation. Besides, the way some folks were eyeing him, like he was Benedict Arnold, meant going anywhere near Savannah would only throw more fuel on the fire.

After grabbing a bottle of water that Sadie had stashed under the table, he went straight to the source of the commotion.

Gently, he touched Thelma's arm. She swung to face him with bloodlust in her eyes. She couldn't have been more than ten years older than him, but bitterness had aged her beyond her years.

"Here," he said, uncapping the bottle and offering it to her. "Why don't you sit down and have a few sips? It might help calm you."

"Calm me? I'm not some silly hysterical woman looking for drama. Is that what you think?"

"Nope. Don't recall saying so either." He smiled and held out the water again. "I just thought you could use something to drink."

Thelma hesitated, breathing hard, her face red and tear streaked. At least she'd stopped shouting. She accepted the bottle and as she sipped from it, he risked a look in Savannah's direction, hoping she understood he wasn't consorting with the enemy.

Her head was bowed and Sadie and Rachel were speaking quietly to her. Around the room, people were griping about one thing or another; how could Savannah have fooled them, why had she pretended to be a tourist, why hadn't she identified herself right off. That she was a spy for Twin Creeks seemed to be a popular theory. A trio of gray-haired, grandmotherly types were texting so fast, it was a wonder their thumbs didn't stiffen up. Probably trying to scoop each other. Under different circumstances, it would've given him a good laugh.

"You don't understand what it's like to be divorced and alone. It's not easy," Thelma muttered, searching through her purse.

"I do. And you're right. It isn't easy."

She pulled out a tissue and blinked up at him. "Are you divorced?"

Mike nodded.

"How long?"

He stopped to think. "About eight years now."

"I've seen you before," she said, squinting at him.

"Probably at the market or hardware store. Our ranch is a ways from town."

She looked down and dabbed at her eyes. "Thank you," she said, clutching the water. "For being so kind. I can't believe I made such a scene. They'll be talking about this for weeks."

"Nah, you know how folks are around here. They'll find something juicier to gossip about by supper time."

She glanced up with a tentative smile then caught sight of Savannah and scowled again.

"Don't worry about Savannah," Mike said. "She'll be fine."

Thelma stared at him as if he'd committed an act of high treason. "You think I care about her? This whole thing is her fault." She glared at Savannah. "Strutting up there like a damn peacock. Announcing who she is like she's proud of herself. Acting like her mamma wasn't the biggest tramp—"

"That's enough." Mike didn't raise his voice, but his stern tone got Thelma's attention. "Savannah was fourteen years old when she was forced to pack up and leave the only home she'd ever known. She was just a kid. Do you have children, Thelma?" He paused, waiting for his words to sink in. But she wasn't quick to let go of her anger. "Savannah was a victim, too."

Thelma blinked, her eyes slowly filling with shame and regret. "I'm—I didn't stop to think," she murmured then cupped a hand over her mouth.

The room had grown quiet.

Sadly, it didn't take long for the rumblings to resume.

Mike had raised his voice at the end, just enough to get everyone's attention. "Tell me something…all of you people who are so quick to judge…are you all prepared to pay for the sins of your parents?" He looked at each of the more vocal agitators. "How about your children—you expect them to pay for yours?"

Despite the sheepish expressions, Mike fought to control his temper. If he heard just one more person mutter about the apple not falling far from *that* tree, he was going to lose it.

"Well, hell, Barnett, it ain't no surprise you'd stick up for her," someone in the back said. "She sent her fiancé packing so she could take up with you."

Mike thought he recognized the voice and turned to look at Lawrence Peabody as a smattering of agreement rippled through the crowd. "Come on, folks," Mike said. "That guy wasn't her fiancé. You all can't be that ignorant."

The indignant gasps made him sigh.

"Please…" Savannah got to her feet. "Don't—"

"Mike's right, you bunch of sorry jackasses," Sadie said, cutting her off and glaring pointedly at Lawrence, Jasper and Earl. "I can't figure out if you're being hardheaded or if you're just plain stupid."

"Sadie, Mike, please." Savannah's voice was shaky and her face was blotchy, but she tried to smile. "It's okay."

"No." Mike shook his head. For her sake, he should probably shut up, but he couldn't hold back. "It's not okay. I defended this town, all of you people—at first I thought it was a bad idea for Savannah to tell you who she was. I advised her against it, but she needed closure and she's had a lot to overcome. She didn't have to take this job, and she certainly didn't have to go to all this effort trying to help Blackfoot Falls.

"So, I changed my way of thinking. I swore you'd never blame her for what her mother did. I tried to convince her that you were kind, fair-minded folks. That you would help her put that painful part of her past behind her.

"I thought I knew you. You folks helped me and mine through some hard times. We've always helped each other when we were able. I love this community, and I've been so proud of what we stood for. But now, I'm deeply ashamed of it. She was a kid. And her world fell apart, and now it's falling apart again for something she had no control over."

Thelma, tissue in hand and her cheeks pink, stood up next to Mike. But she didn't face the crowd. Instead, she looked right at Savannah. "I'm very sorry for what I said. I was wrong to blame you. And I was wrong to be so ugly, no matter what."

Savannah's red eyes looked as bad as Thelma's. "No apology is necessary."

The older woman shook her head. "It most definitely is."

Earl, who'd sneaked closer to the door, coughed. "Apologize for the truth? That's a bunch of bunk."

Savannah seemed to shrink even more, which Mike hadn't thought possible. All he wanted to do was hold her tight and take her far away. He knew that most of these folks had cried out in her defense—had never blamed her—but he doubted that was what Savannah would recall.

It didn't help that Avery, Jasper and Lawrence all pushed off from against the wall, standing with hands on hips, like they'd been the ones assaulted. Idiots.

"Okay, that's it," Sadie said, leaving Rachel to stand by Savannah. "You jackasses need to leave right now. I mean it. As far as I'm concerned, there's going to be some new rules about who's welcome at town meetings."

The room quieted, except for the old troublemakers stuttering their objections.

"We got rights," Jasper said. "Just 'cause we tell the truth don't mean—"

"Get out," Sadie said, except this time it was a command that reverberated against the walls.

Several of the merchants stood, staring daggers at those still complaining. Then Kevin, the motel manager, turned to Savannah. "I, for one, think your business ideas have a great deal of merit, and I'm willing to help form a committee in whatever area you think we need it."

"Hear! Hear!" said someone Mike couldn't see.

"I'm volunteering, too," Kylie said. "I'll do everything I can to make this town all it can be." Then she turned to Savannah with a gentle smile.

"Thank you," Savannah said, her own smile quivering. After the worst of the crowd had left, the place emptied out quietly. But most all of them seemed to need to take one final look at Savannah, which wasn't helping.

Savannah sniffed and took a step away from the table.

Mike moved toward the back, making sure not to block anyone's exit, ready to shut the door when they were all gone. He didn't know what Savannah wanted to do. But he truly had lost a lot of faith in his community today, and he wasn't going to count on a single thing.

He thought back to that day Savannah had told him he was one of her best memories of Blackfoot Falls. It was very easy to imagine the wound that had just been reopened and the scar she'd bear from it. And when all was said and done, he had no idea how he'd come out of this. Would she still think of him fondly, or would he end up lumped into the pain that had just been brought down on her?

SAVANNAH STUFFED EVERYTHING within reach into her briefcase. At the last minute, she remembered to leave out the revised report for Sadie. Her hands were still shaking, but thankfully Rachel had packed up her computer for her.

Mike had also offered to help, but Sadie convinced him to go get some fresh air and cool off. Apparently, she'd never seem him so angry.

It was Savannah's fault. She'd told herself coming here was strictly about closure, but that wasn't true. A big part of her had wanted to prove something to this town...say, hey, look at me, aren't I awesome? What a joke. She looked like a fool. What she regretted most, though, was pitting Mike against his neighbors.

Trying to sound as professional as possible, she said, "Tell you what, Mayor, let's give everyone some time to calm down, say about a week, then I'll send Nina to finish the presentation. How does that sound?"

Sadie snorted a laugh.

"It's only fair." She owed it to them for her colossal lapse in judgment.

"You're a better woman than me, Savannah." Sadie patted her arm. "You've done more than enough. Going over to Twin Creeks and Greensville and all… I know this will be hard to believe, but most of these folks understand and appreciate what you've done. It's always the loudmouthed idiots that ruin things for the rest of us."

"It's fine," Savannah said, trying to hide a surge of relief. "I hope you can forgive me for dropping that bomb. I thought it would help if they knew I do understand life here." She sighed. "Which I obviously don't, given what happened."

"You hush. There's nothing to forgive." Sadie sandwiched Savannah's cold hand between her warm palms. "I remember you now, and you've got every right to be damn proud of yourself. Does my heart good to see how far you've come. And I'll tell you something else," she said, leaning closer. "I thoroughly enjoyed that lecture Mike gave those old coots."

"Amen," Rachel said.

The mayor frowned at her. "I was whispering for a reason."

"Better learn to do it softer, then."

Sadie chuckled. "Rachel lays into them every town meeting. They've come to expect it. But I've never seen Mike get so riled. He's the most easygoing man I know. Normally, he tends to keep to himself. But I guarantee he's made a lot of people think today, about more than just this." She glanced toward the door. "Let's hope it sticks. He's waiting for you just outside. Poked his head in twice now."

Savannah drew in a deep breath and nodded, not sure she was ready to face him. If only she'd listened to his warning. But, no. In the end, her ego had won. "Thanks," she said, looking from Sadie to Rachel. "Both of you. For everything."

Rachel came around the table and hugged her. "I still can't believe I didn't recognize you," she said, leaning back then squeezing Savannah's arms before releasing her. "I'm glad you have Mike. You're in good hands."

"He's just—we're not—" Savannah gave up. Why repeat herself? Why postpone the inevitable? She saw Mike peek in again, just as her phone rang.

Porter's ringtone.

Savannah winced.

"Go ahead and answer, we'll give you some privacy." Sadie looped an arm through Rachel's and steered her toward the door. "Take your time and don't worry about locking up. I'll see to it later. And call if you need anything."

Savannah had no intention of answering the call now, but she smiled her gratitude, anxious for them to leave so she could be alone. Even for just a minute.

Chapter Twenty

Mike must've thought she was on the phone because it took him a while to duck inside. "All clear?" His warm, familiar smile lightened her heart. Not that she deserved it.

Nodding, she managed to return the smile as she picked up her briefcase and laptop. They both felt so much heavier than they had earlier.

"Here." He hurried over to her and took the laptop case.

She held on to her briefcase when he tried to grab it as well, for no other reason than he'd done too much for her already. Another layer of guilt would crush her. God, she didn't even know where to begin.

"I moved the truck closer." He held the door then turned off the lights. "We're going to the motel, right?"

"You shouldn't be neglecting the ranch for me." As she stepped onto the sidewalk, she slipped on her sunglasses and checked both sides.

A group of chatty women was leaving the diner halfway down the next block while a pair of older men were busy inspecting their fishing poles outside Abe's Variety.

"I pretty much chased everyone home," Mike said with a short laugh.

Her mouth was dry. She couldn't swallow. It was so like him to try to make her feel better, which only made her feel worse. Mike was the last person on earth she'd ever wanted to hurt.

"I can't begin to tell you how sorry I am," she whispered, holding back tears. Although, why worry about being professional now?

"Savannah?"

She turned and only then realized that he'd stopped. She'd almost walked right by his truck.

He held the passenger door open for her, and she climbed in.

The second he was behind the wheel, he took one of her hands in his. "Listen, you have nothing to apologize for. You didn't do anything wrong. Hell, the only reason I regret getting steamed is because I had a lot more to say but I let my temper get in the way."

"Mike, I appreciate you trying to protect me but—" Her voice broke.

Oh, God.

She pulled her hand away and held it up, pleading for silence while she collected herself.

It was true. Mike had tried to protect her from the very beginning and when she'd ignored his warning, he'd defended her anyway. Savannah couldn't think of a single person who'd ever put themselves on the line trying to protect her. Not even her own mother. Certainly not her father. No one.

Except Mike.

And the gut-wrenching knowledge of how she'd repaid his kindness was the thing that was going to do her in. Humiliation rose in her like a wave, pressing on her lungs and throat. He'd be the hot topic for weeks. Eventually the gossip would turn elsewhere, but that didn't mean resentment toward him wouldn't linger.

"Savannah." He reclaimed her hand, warming it between

his work-roughened palms. "No one is blaming you for what happened today," he said, his eyes dark pools of concern. "Well, except maybe you." He smiled with a brief flicker of humor. "By the way, your text made my day."

Confused, she frowned. "My text?"

"A week's vacation?"

Savannah was speechless. Surely he didn't think she could stay now. After what had happened?

"I hope you've given some thought to staying at the ranch with me. There's an extra room, if that's what you want. You can unwind, go to the creek, watch the sunrise and sunset every day. Just chill. Or I can put you to work." He smiled again, his thumb idly rubbing the back of her hand. "You wouldn't have to see anyone, other than Chip, and not even him if you don't want to."

She shook her head, astonished that she could be the least bit tempted. "How could you want to have anything to do with me after what I did?"

His thumb stilled. "Come on, Savannah. I know you're smarting right now, but once you've settled and you're more clearheaded, I promise you'll see that none of it was your fault."

Oh, she didn't doubt he believed that, but he was wrong. "Did you know Thelma was going to be there?"

His hurt expression took her to a new level of shame.

"Of course you didn't. Please, just ignore me…" She looked away. "Can we go to the motel now?"

Mike started the truck and they drove in silence.

Savannah's brain was far from quiet, though. She had no idea what to say. If the drive wasn't so brief she might've checked for a flight out this evening. But no, she really wasn't that big of a coward.

Perhaps her last thoughtless, hurtful remark had taken

care of the problem. He probably couldn't wait to get rid of her.

He parked in a spot close to the entrance, opened his door and hesitated. "Are you already packed?"

"Pretty much."

"Okay to come up with you now, or should I give you a few minutes?"

"Come on up." She hadn't figured out how to tell him, with any grace at all, that she was leaving as soon as possible. At least in the room, they'd be assured of privacy and if she cried, it wouldn't matter. Her embarrassment had already reached a level she could barely stand.

As soon as he shut the door behind them, Mike pulled her into his arms. The hug was like being given a lifeline, a safe harbor. The tighter he held her, the more she trembled.

"I've been wanting to do this all afternoon," he whispered, his warm breath on her neck so soothing. So undeserved. "I can't wait to steal you away. Get us out of town, back to the quiet of the ranch. You can watch all the movies you want or crawl into bed, where I'll bring you tea and éclairs—"

She stopped him with her lips. A sweet kiss, meant to be a thank-you, an apology, a wish that things could be different. Mike turned it into something else entirely. It wasn't hard to read. He wanted her to stay. He was sorry for what had happened. He wished he could change the past and probably the future.

Just as she was about to pull back, to tell him her plans, her cell phone rang. It wasn't Porter's tone. But it was work. Most likely Ron, who she had forgotten about.

"I have to take that," she said. "It's—"

"Work. I know." He let his arms drop. Her hand lingered on his forearm until she had to grab the call before it went to voice mail.

"Hello?"

"Where the hell have you been?" Ron sounded frantic. "I've been trying to get you all day."

"I'm sorry. The presentation went in a direction I hadn't anticipated."

"Next time I tell you it's urgent, try to get back to me sooner rather than later."

"What happened?" Her gaze shot to Mike, who nodded toward the door with a questioning look. Savannah shook her head but turned slightly away so she could concentrate.

"You're not going to like it."

Her stomach tightened. "Just tell me."

"Look, this isn't easy for me to admit." Ron cleared his throat. "Porter and I go way back. Way back, and he was really surprised that after two years you decided to go back in the field. So he asked me to go along with you."

"Wait. You were spying—"

"I wouldn't put it—" Ron sighed. "Basically, yes."

She huffed and when she breathed in again, it stoked the anger coiling in her belly. "Unbelievable!"

"You're pissed. I get it. I would be, too. But I'm taking a big risk here. I know you can mess me up with Porter and get me fired. Obviously, I hope you don't. In any case, I was supposed to stick with you, but I hated that he'd even asked me, so I took off. Then you decided to take vacation and Porter freaked out.

"Look, I'm sorry I went along with it. You work hard and you've always been straight with me. Throw me under the bus if you want, but I figured I owed you. And hell, I should have flat out told Porter no."

She sat with this new information for a minute, her thoughts bouncing all over the place. "Does anyone else in the office know about me and Porter?"

"I don't think so." He cleared his throat, and she braced

herself for the next awful thing. "I hope you're not going to keep seeing him."

Savannah let out a short, incredulous laugh.

"Oh, hell, I'm probably going to get fired anyway. I really do like you, Savannah, and I mean this as a friend. But you're not the only one."

She didn't understand. At first. "Oh, God."

"I'm sorry, and this won't be any easier to hear, but he's never going to leave his wife. Like I said, Porter and I are old friends, but… Hell, you're too good for him."

Her thumb hit the disconnect button before she could utter another word.

Stricken with a brand-new wave of humiliation and shame, she turned to find Mike. But he wasn't in the room. Then she noticed the bathroom door was closed when it hadn't been earlier.

What she didn't know was how much he'd heard. Probably enough that he wouldn't have a single complaint about her leaving as soon as possible. In fact, she connected to the airline and booked an evening flight.

The moment she hung up, Mike exited the bathroom. From the look on his face, she knew he'd gotten an earful. Before she told him face-to-face that she was leaving, she wanted to tell him she was sorry, but the words stuck in her throat.

MIKE HAD KNOWN the moment he'd lost her. It wasn't this afternoon at the presentation, although that alone must've made her want to bolt. Having finally gotten closure at the cabin, Savannah had been dragged straight into the dirt of public shame.

But it was the phone call. The news, whatever it had been, about Porter.

It made so damn much sense that she'd need to go back

to Denver, to someone like her boss. Someone who validated her, who made her feel special. And who didn't know all her secrets. It hardly mattered that she didn't have feelings for the man. Porter was rich, important, powerful and he wanted Savannah. That made her a hot ticket in everyone's eyes. Mike didn't even blame her. It all made sense, in a sad way.

"Mike," Savannah said, her voice tight, her eyes telling him what he already knew. "I'm sorry. That was about work, and my career is in a pretty precarious place at the moment. I won't be able to stay the week, although it was a wonderful idea that I would've loved. But things have gotten more complicated."

Just like the presentation that had gone in a direction she hadn't anticipated. He supposed both things were true. She hadn't counted on connecting with someone who remembered her. Who she'd bared her soul to. That her position was precarious wasn't even a lie. At least, he didn't think so. "That's…disappointing."

Which wasn't a lie either.

He'd known she wasn't the woman he needed. The wife he needed. In one respect, she was a lot like Ellen. He didn't know why he hadn't made the connection before, but for the same reason Ellen couldn't have been satisfied with being a ranch wife, he doubted Savannah could either. She needed a man who made her feel like somebody.

"I'm sorry it couldn't have worked out," she said, stepping closer to him. "You've been so amazing, showing me nothing but kindness. And frankly—" Her voice broke. "I'll never forget you. Not ever."

Despite what his brain said, his heart jumped hard and he pulled her into his arms. "Stay, Savannah. Just another day."

She sagged against him, burying her face against his neck.

"Give yourself some space and time," he murmured against her hair. Her body was soft and warm and seeking comfort that he was more than willing to give. Even if that meant just holding her all night.

Her breathy sigh teased the skin exposed by his shirt. "I can't." She drew back, and he let her go. A sad smile touched her lips. "I'll miss you."

"Me too." His voice sounded hoarse. "What time is your flight?"

Her face paled. "Please understand." She moved back a step. "I'm going to ask Sadie to take me."

Mike hadn't even seen that blow coming.

Chapter Twenty-One

Savannah had been in Denver for two days, but she was still exhausted. She sat in her windowless office, staring at the photograph of a sunset she'd just hung on her wall. The photographer had captured the sun just as it had seemingly burst into red flames over a range of jagged mountain peaks. It was a beautiful work of art. But it didn't grab her like the sunsets she and Mike had watched together.

With a sigh, she leaned back in her chair. Clearly, being with Mike had had a lot to do with it. Everything had been more enjoyable with him. Simple things like taking a drive or stopping for a cup of coffee. He made her feel comfortable and more herself.

Ironic, really, since he was the only person who possessed a true perspective of her evolution, from a timid, neglected child to a reasonably successful woman. He'd seen the shabby old cabin, had known of her parents' bickering and her dad's vile temper. Mike had guessed at some of the other unpleasant parts of her childhood and oddly, she didn't regret having filled in some of the blanks.

Yes, Mike knew about most of the skeletons in her closet. And he hadn't judged her or pitied her once. No words could describe how much she appreciated that.

Studying the photograph, her mood took a dive. It was supposed to cheer her up, remind her of the good times with Mike. Not depress her. Thinking about how much she'd paid for it sent her spirits down another notch. She'd had no business splurging like that, considering she might be without a job soon.

No, Porter wouldn't be that petty.

Would he?

Just because she'd told him this thing between them, whatever it had become, wasn't working for her?

Guess she wouldn't know until he arrived on Monday.

She needed a stiff drink, but she'd settle for coffee.

Savannah rose, stopping to adjust the frame on her way out of her office. Crazy as it seemed, she now hoped Porter hadn't filed for divorce, that he wasn't even separated, just as Ron had implied. Yes, it made her all the more a fool. But it also bought her some time to find another job if it came down to that. If Porter still cared about his wife, he wouldn't want this thing to blow up and go public.

She made her way to the break room, ignoring the looks and whispers of her coworkers. They'd been at it since yesterday. She might as well be living in Blackfoot Falls.

The thought somehow struck her as funny. It hadn't lasted long before the sick feeling in her stomach was back. She didn't know what the gossip was about, since she was fairly confident Ron hadn't said anything about her and Porter. Ron had reason to be concerned about his own job, though she wouldn't say anything about what he'd confided.

She groaned when she saw the carafe was nearly empty.

"You want to rethink that vacation?" Jeanine asked, coming up behind her as she reached for the filters.

"Want the last cup?"

"No thanks. I'll wait." Jeanine laughed. "You know you can throw that out. A fresh cup won't break our budget."

"You're right." Savannah poured it into the sink. "That was incredibly freeing."

Jeanine was already getting the coffee out of the cabinet.

The woman hadn't just been Savannah's mentor, she was a friend. And this wasn't the first look of concern she'd given Savannah. That Jeanine was the regional manager and Savannah's immediate boss made their relationship tricky.

After filling the carafe with water, Savannah couldn't stand it. "Any idea what's going on with the rumor mill?" she asked, knowing it was a long shot. Jeanine hated and discouraged gossip. "Somehow I get the feeling I'm the hot topic."

"Well, I don't know for sure," Jeanine said, measuring out the coffee. "I think it might have to do with Porter coming straight here."

"And that relates to me how?"

Jeanine's small, tolerant smile shot down any hope Savannah harbored that no one knew about her and Porter. She rubbed the back of her neck then watched as Jeanine continued making the coffee.

Savannah glanced back to make sure they were alone. "Am I going to be fired?" she asked softly.

"No." Jeanine's brows lifted in surprise. "Why would you think that? Because of the Blackfoot Falls job? The client is happy."

So, maybe Savannah was wrong and no one knew about Porter. But then, why the stares? "After everyone leaves, would you have a few minutes for me?"

"I always have time for you, kiddo, you know that. We can talk right now."

"Um, it's a closed-door kind of thing."

"Ah, yes, nothing the grapevine likes more."

"Uh-huh." Savannah paused when Valerie from accounting walked in. "Coffee's not ready yet."

"Just getting something out of the fridge," Valerie said, glancing from Jeanine to Savannah.

They waited until she left the room, and then Jeanine said, "The place will clear at the stroke of five. Come on in whenever you feel comfortable." On her way out, she gave Savannah an encouraging smile and a pat on the arm.

She was so lucky that Jeanine had her back. Which didn't give Savannah free rein to overshare. No, in the next two hours she had to really think about how much she wanted to tell the woman.

At least it gave her something to do, other than daydream about Mike.

MIKE SWORE AS he slammed the front door. He'd been an idiot and had forgotten to check the gas in the ATV. He'd had to abandon it three miles from home, and Chip was off today.

The long walk back had given him far too much time to think. Not that the subject had changed since Savannah had flown out of his life five days ago. It hadn't mattered what he'd been up to—she was never far from his thoughts. Either it was something they had done together, eaten together, laughed at together, or something he wanted her to see, eat or laugh at with him. And that was just the G-rated stuff.

Damn, what was happening to him? They'd been together for less than a week. It made no sense that he couldn't get past this…thing. This longing.

Especially because he knew she wasn't right for him. She belonged in Denver, and he belonged on the ranch. The twain weren't about to meet.

Maybe he should go to Florida for Thanksgiving. Although that could be a particularly tough time on the ranch—late November was notorious for heavy snowfall.

He sat down on the couch then wished he'd gotten a beer from the fridge. Today's mistake certainly wasn't his first. Maybe if he talked to Savannah. He'd called her once, to make sure she'd gotten home okay, but his message had gone to voice mail, and she hadn't called back.

That was forty-eight hours ago.

Now he was getting worried. He'd been worried since the presentation, but this was on a whole new level. She might have been fired, might have gotten in over her head with her boss and dammit, she'd been in terrible shape when they'd said goodbye.

But the truth was, she could be completely happy, having won the heart of the wealthy and prominent Porter. Or just glad to be back in her real world.

Sure, they'd had a great time together, but it hadn't been love.

At least, it hadn't been for her.

THANK GOD PORTER had waited until after-hours to come to Savannah's office. He seemed puzzled that a window view hadn't come with her promotion, but his concern for her quickly changed to concern for himself. "I don't understand. You know it's not simple for a man in my position to get a divorce. You wouldn't want me to lose everything, would you?"

"Then my decision should make you happy. I don't need you to get a divorce. I'm sorry, but I've already explained, this long-distance thing isn't working for me. And you being married is a complication I can't ignore."

"Is that it? The reason it's not working for you? Because I swear—"

"Don't. That's not the only reason."

"It's a guy, isn't it? What, some rich rancher in Montana? What did he promise you? Tell me what you want, and it's yours." Sitting on the edge of her desk, he ran a hand through his blond hair and looked at her as if she were the only thing in the world that could make him complete.

Yeah, her and all his other women.

Reluctantly, Jeanine, who'd known the Burkes a long time, had confirmed what Ron had said. That Porter had had his share of affairs. How he'd managed to keep his indiscretions a secret, Savannah couldn't begin to guess. Not that it mattered to her. She'd known they were over before she'd left Blackfoot Falls.

She stood. "It's late, and I—"

Porter closed his hands around her upper arms, and it reminded her so much of Mike that she squirmed out of the hold. "What, now you don't even like me touching you?"

Ah. Finally. She understood why he was working so hard for such a small return on his investment. Porter didn't care for being dumped. Although she'd bet a year's salary he got off on being the dumper. All of this must be just a game for him. Wins and more wins. To lose…unbearable.

She walked from behind her desk, away from him, across the small room so she could look at the sunset on her wall. "I appreciate the time we've spent together, and I'm still very flattered, but it's over."

His lips curved in an unattractive smile. "What if I were to rush the divorce?"

She said a silent thanks to Mike Burnett for helping her be strong enough to not think twice. "Nope. Sorry."

The smile disappeared, but his unhappiness with her didn't. How had she never seen how cold his blue eyes could be? Or maybe she had but chose to ignore it. Funny how she'd gone back looking for perspective in her past only to find it in her future.

"You're joking, right?" Porter's pleading had vanished. His voice was as dismissive as her father's used to be when he wasn't winning an argument. "Well, fine. But maybe next time, try not to be such an obvious tease. I'm not saying your work wasn't good, but…"

"My work?"

"What?" he said, acting shocked. "Yeah, the report you did was decent, and they liked you in Buffalo Flats, or wherever. Although it wasn't one of your more lucrative deals."

"Right," she said. "Thanks for the career advice, but I actually have somewhere to be in just a few minutes, so…"

"Sure thing," he said, opening her office door. "Be my guest."

She pulled her purse out of her bottom drawer and got her coat off the hook. When she walked out the door, she left him with her very best smile.

He didn't return it.

And she didn't give one damn.

SEVENTEEN MORE DAYS to go until Savannah was unemployed. With no unemployment benefits, since it had been her decision. Right after seeing Porter, she'd given her notice. She could have given two weeks, but that would have left Jeanine in a bind, so they settled on three.

After her walk at lunch, and despite her warm coat, she felt chilled to the bone. The first thing she did was get some tea from the break room. The second thing she did was cross off another day on her desk calendar.

She had savings. One thing she'd learned from her mother was how to budget and ever since her first job, she'd put aside 10 percent of her salary, so she would be okay while she figured out how to make her next move.

In the meantime, she had some reports to go over. Taking one last sip of peppermint tea, she opened the first file. Before she could get past the introduction, there was a knock on her open door.

Expecting her assistant, she gasped as she looked up. "Mike." It was as if she'd been hit by a falling star. Nothing could have prepared her for that face, that man, standing right in front of her. "What are you doing here?"

He had his Stetson in his hand, but instead of his jeans and Western shirt, he had on khakis and a sweater underneath his jacket. He stepped inside the room, his gaze worried. "I'm not here to bother you or anything, but I think we're still friends, and when I didn't hear from you... I just wanted to make sure you were all right."

"You didn't get my call?"

He looked shocked. "When?"

"This morning."

"Savannah, it's been two weeks since you left. You didn't return my call, never got in touch." He pulled out his cell phone. "I turned it off this morning before I got on the plane." He did look tired and stressed. "Should I listen to the message?"

"I can tell you," she said, standing up. She walked from behind her desk but before she did anything else, she shut her office door, tempted to lock it.

When she turned, Mike was close. She got a nice whiff of his woodsy leather scent, which she'd missed more than seemed possible. "I'm so sorry I left the way I did. And I'm sorry I didn't call you back right away. But every day since the moment I got on that plane, I've thought about you. About how easy it was to be with you, and how I'd missed out on something I'd regret forever."

"What, you mean me?"

Tears welled and she had no intention of stopping them. "I'm not surprised that you flew here to find out if I'm okay. Because that's the...the..."

Now she'd done it. She wasn't just teary, she was sobbing. His arms were around her, and she was gripping his sweater so tightly she'd probably rip it, and it was Mike. And he was really here.

"It's okay, honey," he said, so softly right by her ear. "You're all right. Still beautiful, and still the best woman I know."

She cried harder, and oh, damn, she was going to mess up his jacket.

"Shh. Savannah. You're safe. I've got you."

Of course, that didn't help. "Why was it so easy to shrug off Porter's ugly words, but I crumble like an old cookie when you walk into the room. I don't even know why I can't stop."

Oddly, saying that out loud helped. She leaned back, although he didn't let her go completely. His hands were still on her arms.

"I need a tissue."

He reached over and picked up the small box sitting on her desk. She laughed as she plucked four, wondering if they would be enough.

"Great, I'm wiping off more makeup than tears."

"Doesn't matter. You're still beautiful."

"Yeah. Sure. Listen," she said, then paused to blow her nose.

He grinned.

She shook her head. "I didn't mean that. I meant to say that I'm really, truly fine. Better than that, actually. Because I don't care one wit about what the people in Blackfoot Falls think about me. Or the people in Denver, for that matter. I'm not spending another minute wasting time rehashing the past, including the fact that I've given my notice and will be leaving this job in seventeen days. I keep thinking about how I felt at the ranch. At the creek. Don't take this the wrong way, but it wasn't all about you. Mostly it was, but honestly, I don't believe I belong here. Going back reminded me I need wide open spaces, lots of grass and trees. Time to watch the sun rise and set."

"Really?"

She nodded, smiling right back at him. "I've been thinking about what I want to do. And it's not that different from working here, except I would be an independent consultant."

"Yeah?"

"Yeah. How are you? I didn't even ask—"

"I'm fine. Better now, but I'm good. Still trying to get back into my old routine."

"Oh, is something wrong?"

"Not anymore," he said, smiling. "I was actually thinking that the flight between Kalispell and Denver isn't half-bad."

"Oh, Mike." She pulled him close and kissed him hard.

He reacted in the best possible way—by kissing her back with so much passion she almost melted. Thank goodness she'd shut the door, because she wanted his touch. Her own hands went under his jacket as she pressed against him.

His moan slipped between her lips and straight down to her heart. And maybe a bit lower, too. How had she walked away from him?

It was Mike who pulled back this time. Not far. And he still hadn't let go. "I couldn't stop thinking about you. Not for a single day. Made a lot of mistakes on the ranch. Chip's been mooing at me, telling me to stop with the big cow eyes. Annoying little shit."

Savannah laughed. "I think they're more like a puppy dog's than a cow's."

His smile warmed her from head to toe. "As long as they're looking at you, I don't care what kind they are."

She wiped her cheeks again. "You know, ever since we visited all those smaller towns, I've been thinking I'd like to try and tap that market. I could look at the towns around northwestern Montana. You know. To start."

He was looking at her with hope and confusion. "Is that your way of telling me you might be making a move?"

She nodded. "I can't stop thinking about you and what life could be, if I let it." She breathed in. "What do you think?"

His smile was wide enough to reach across the whole state as he picked her up and kissed her until it was time to watch the sunset.

* * * * *

*If you enjoyed this story,
be sure to pick up the earlier books
in the* MADE IN MONTANA *miniseries.
Check out* STEALING THE COWBOY'S HEART
from Harlequin Western Romance or
SIZZLING SUMMER NIGHTS *and*
HOT WINTER NIGHTS
from Harlequin Blaze!

HOME on the RANCH

YES! Please send me the **Home on the Ranch Collection** in Larger Print. This collection begins with 3 FREE books and 2 FREE gifts in the first shipment. Along with my 3 free books, I'll also get the next 4 books from the Home on the Ranch Collection, in LARGER PRINT, which I may either return and owe nothing, or keep for the low price of $5.24 U.S./ $5.89 CDN each plus $2.99 for shipping and handling per shipment*. If I decide to continue, about once a month for 8 months I will get 6 or 7 more books, but will only need to pay for 4. That means 2 or 3 books in every shipment will be FREE! If I decide to keep the entire collection, I'll have paid for only 32 books because 19 books are FREE! I understand that accepting the 3 free books and gifts places me under no obligation to buy anything. I can always return a shipment and cancel at any time. My free books and gifts are mine to keep no matter what I decide.

268 HCN 3760 468 HCN 3760

Name	(PLEASE PRINT)	
Address		Apt. #
City	State/Prov.	Zip/Postal Code

Signature (if under 18, a parent or guardian must sign)

Mail to the **Reader Service:**

IN U.S.A.: P.O. Box 1867, Buffalo, NY. 14240-1867
IN CANADA: P.O. Box 609, Fort Erie, Ontario L2A 5X3

* Terms and prices subject to change without notice. Prices do not include applicable taxes. Sales tax applicable in NY. Canadian residents will be charged applicable taxes. This offer is limited to one order per household. All orders subject to approval. Credit or debit balances in a customer's account(s) may be offset by any other outstanding balance owed by or to the customer. Please allow 3 to 4 weeks for delivery. Offer available while quantities last. Offer not available to Quebec residents.

HRCBPA18

Get 2 Free Books,
Plus 2 Free Gifts—
just for trying the Reader Service!

HARLEQUIN *Presents*®

YES! Please send me 2 FREE Harlequin Presents® novels and my 2 FREE gifts (gifts are worth about $10 retail). After receiving them, if I don't wish to receive any more books, I can return the shipping statement marked "cancel." If I don't cancel, I will receive 6 brand-new novels every month and be billed just $4.55 each for the regular-print edition or $5.55 each for the larger-print edition in the U.S., or $5.49 each for the regular-print edition or $5.99 each for the larger-print edition in Canada. That's a saving of at least 11% off the cover price! It's quite a bargain! Shipping and handling is just 50¢ per book in the U.S. and 75¢ per book in Canada*. I understand that accepting the 2 free books and gifts places me under no obligation to buy anything. I can always return a shipment and cancel at any time. The free books and gifts are mine to keep no matter what I decide.

Please check one: ☐ Harlequin Presents® Regular-Print   ☐ Harlequin Presents® Larger-Print
                       (106/306 HDN GMWK)   (176/376 HDN GMWK)

Name	(PLEASE PRINT)
Address	Apt. #
City State/Prov.	Zip/Postal Code

Signature (if under 18, a parent or guardian must sign)

Mail to the **Reader Service:**
IN U.S.A.: P.O. Box 1341, Buffalo, NY 14240-8531
IN CANADA: P.O. Box 603, Fort Erie, Ontario L2A 5X3

Want to try two free books from another series?
Call 1-800-873-8635 or visit www.ReaderService.com.

* Terms and prices subject to change without notice. Prices do not include applicable taxes. Sales tax applicable in N.Y. Canadian residents will be charged applicable taxes. Offer not valid in Quebec. This offer is limited to one order per household. Books received may not be as shown. Not valid for current subscribers to Harlequin Presents books. All orders subject to approval. Credit or debit balances in a customer's account(s) may be offset by any other outstanding balance owed by or to the customer. Please allow 4 to 6 weeks for delivery. Offer available while quantities last.

Your Privacy—The Reader Service is committed to protecting your privacy. Our Privacy Policy is available online at www.ReaderService.com or upon request from the Reader Service.

We make a portion of our mailing list available to reputable third parties that offer products we believe may interest you. If you prefer that we not exchange your name with third parties, or if you wish to clarify or modify your communication preferences, please visit us at www.ReaderService.com/consumerschoice or write to us at Reader Service Preference Service, P.O. Box 9062, Buffalo, NY 14240-9062. Include your complete name and address.

Get 2 Free Books,
Plus 2 Free Gifts—
just for trying the **Reader Service!**

YES! Please send me 2 FREE Harlequin® Romance Larger-Print novels and my 2 FREE gifts (gifts are worth about $10 retail). After receiving them, if I don't wish to receive any more books, I can return the shipping statement marked "cancel." If I don't cancel, I will receive 4 brand-new novels every month and be billed just $5.34 per book in the U.S. or $5.74 per book in Canada. That's a savings of at least 15% off the cover price! It's quite a bargain! Shipping and handling is just 50¢ per book in the U.S. and 75¢ per book in Canada*. I understand that accepting the 2 free books and gifts places me under no obligation to buy anything. I can always return a shipment and cancel at any time. The free books and gifts are mine to keep no matter what I decide.

119/319 HDN GMWL

Name   (PLEASE PRINT)

Address   Apt. #

City   State/Prov.   Zip/Postal Code

Signature (if under 18, a parent or guardian must sign)

Mail to the **Reader Service:**
IN U.S.A.: P.O. Box 1341, Buffalo, NY 14240-8531
IN CANADA: P.O. Box 603, Fort Erie, Ontario L2A 5X3
Want to try two free books from another line?
Call 1-800-873-8635 or visit www.ReaderService.com.

*Terms and prices subject to change without notice. Prices do not include applicable taxes. Sales tax applicable in N.Y. Canadian residents will be charged applicable taxes. Offer not valid in Quebec. This offer is limited to one order per household. Books received may not be as shown. Not valid for current subscribers to Harlequin Romance Larger-Print books. All orders subject to approval. Credit or debit balances in a customer's account(s) may be offset by any other outstanding balance owed by or to the customer. Please allow 4 to 6 weeks for delivery. Offer available while quantities last.

Your Privacy—The Reader Service is committed to protecting your privacy. Our Privacy Policy is available online at www.ReaderService.com or upon request from the Reader Service.

We make a portion of our mailing list available to reputable third parties that offer products we believe may interest you. If you prefer that we not exchange your name with third parties, or if you wish to clarify or modify your communication preferences, please visit us at www.ReaderService.com/consumerschoice or write to us at Reader Service Preference Service, P.O. Box 9062, Buffalo, NY 14240-9062. Include your complete name and address.

HRLP17R3

Get 2 Free Books,
Plus 2 Free Gifts –

just for trying the **Reader Service!**